A Baseball Horror Story

AERYN RUDEL

A
Grinning Skull Press
Publication
PO Box 67, Bridgewater, MA 02324

ISBN-13: 978-1-947227-79-8 (paperback)
ISBN: 978-1-947227-80-4 (e-book)

Thanks for making our home beautiful. Let me make you disturbed and freaked out in return :)

DEDICATION

This is for my dad, who gave me baseball.

ACKNOWLEDGMENTS

I'd like to thank the following people for their work, support, and inspiration.

Many thanks to my excellent critique partners Maura Yzmore and Graham Robert Scott for helping me shape the story and turn it into something publishable. Neither are baseball fans, but they convinced me readers don't need to be to enjoy the story. I hope they're right. They usually are.

My wife, Melissa, always tells me my weird ideas are only good weird and something I should pursue. Her unwavering support and love is what drives me to keep writing, keep going, keep believing.

Lastly, I'd like to thank the folks at *Pseudopod* who published another monster/baseball story of mine, giving me hope I might be able to publish another one. Grinning Skull Press clearly thought there was room for more of this kind of mashup, and I am very grateful.

"Pitching is the art of instilling fear."

—Sandy Koufax

May 10th

Know a catcher by his knees, Martin Wagner thought as he taped bags of ice to his. He'd become an expert in the application of cold to torn ligaments and inflamed joints. As he ministered to his aching knees, he watched young men in their prime strut around in perfect injury-free bodies, laughing and joking, utterly confident in their indestructibility. Martin tried not to hate them. Not easy for a thirty-seven-year-old catcher at the ass-end of his career who had to pop two Percocet to even get on the field, let alone play at something resembling a professional level. The aging athlete is a resentful creature.

Martin leaned against his locker. It was too small and too close to the others. Not like the cavernous, walk-in closet-sized joints in the big leagues. But he was not in the big leagues anymore. He'd been relegated to the minors last season, and in the minors, you made do with less. His head brushed the black-and-gray Sacramento Stars uniform hung above his locker. The Stars were a minor-league affiliate of the San Francisco Giants. Not so long ago, he'd worn the black and orange of the big team. Not so long ago, a big-league salary helped alleviate the pain in his knees, back, and neck. League minimum, sure, but that six-hundred grand let him pay his alimony and hang on to enough to live comfortably. Now, exiled to Triple-A, he made a fraction of that. He was two payments behind on his alimony, living in a one-room shit box—he couldn't bring himself to share a place with one of his embryonic teammates—his big-league career a swiftly fading memory. Veronica, his ex, was sympathetic to his predicament and let him slide on the alimony. Her magnanimity somehow made him feel worse about himself. The aging athlete is also a dumping ground for toxic male hang-ups.

"Hey, Wags," said a voice as loud and clear as an angel's trumpet.

Martin turned at the sound of his nickname and saw Justin Bars standing atop the Stars logo in the middle of the locker room. Fresh from the showers, Justin was an umber-skinned demigod. The top prospect for the Giants towered an impressive six-foot-five. Two-hundred-thirty-five pounds of lean, explosive muscle. He could hit a baseball four-hundred feet with an almost contemptuous flick of his mighty wrists, throw a ninety-five-mile-per-hour seed from the center field fence to home plate, and run the ninety feet to first in an astonishing 3.9 seconds. He was handsome, confident, and barring catastrophic injury, he'd get the call up to the big club before season's end.

"What's up, Bars?" said Martin.

"You gave a clinic behind the plate today. I've never

4

seen pitch-framing like that." Standing there in his unabashed nakedness, somehow unaware of his youth and almost supernatural talent, Justin was giving Martin his blessing. The cool kid had spoken, and the others in the locker room nodded in agreement.

Martin forced a smile. "Thanks, man." He should have stopped there, accepted the compliment, and moved on. Instead, his stupid mouth teamed up with his bruised ego and blurted out, "You pick up a thing or two in ten seasons in the show."

"Maybe, but I think that's just talent, bro," Justin replied graciously with a wide, sincere smile. He patted Martin on the shoulder, then moved on to chat with other lesser deities of the pantheon, leaving Martin to marinate in a bitter cocktail of resentment and self-loathing. Martin thought about the bottle of Jack Daniels back at his apartment. He'd been chasing his nightly Percocet with a few shots before bed. He might start early tonight.

Martin hunkered on his stool, a battle-scarred ogre trying to tune out the youthful clamor around him. He was about to reach for his earbuds to drown out all the hope and joy in the room when Mike Embrey pushed through the double doors, coming from the manager's offices. Mike was the bench coach for the Stars, the number two right below the manager. He was a lean, wolfish dude in his early fifties who'd been a halfway decent shortstop in the big leagues. Smart, observant, and well liked, Mike had "big-league manager" written all over him. He spotted Martin and beelined over to him.

"Fuck," Martin said under his breath and pressed his

ice packs more firmly onto his knees. At his age, attention from management rarely meant anything good.

"How're the knees, Wags?" Mike asked, his high, almost musical voice a sharp contrast to his game-worn frame.

Martin looked up at the bench coach and again forced a smile, only this one wasn't quite as labored: at least Mike understood what it was like to get old. "They hurt like a motherfucker. Next stupid question."

Mike grinned. "Asking a catcher about his knees is like asking the Pope for condoms. Stupid, and you already know the answer."

"What's up?" Martin prodded. Best to get whatever shit news Mike had come to deliver.

The humor fell away from Mike's face. "Skip wants to see you."

The Stars manager—or Skipper, or just Skip—was Jorge Vasquez, a quiet man possessed of encyclopedic and hard-earned baseball knowledge. He'd been drafted at sixteen without knowing a word of English, brought from Mexico to the States to play baseball, where he'd excelled as both a player and now as a manager. He, too, had big things in his future.

Martin sighed. His turn to ask a dumb question. "He say what about?"

"Nope, "Mike replied. "Just wants to see you. Now."

Martin stripped the ice pack off his left knee. "Tell him I'll be there in a sec." He somehow kept his voice and hands from shaking. Not bad for a guy facing the end of everything he's known and loved.

Mike opened his mouth like he wanted to say more, maybe offer a word of comfort, then closed it slowly and walked away.

Martin pulled the ice off his right knee, the real asshole of the two, and stood. The joint barked as he struggled into a pair of sweats. He slid on his flip-flops and walked through the sea of bright, young faces. Some of them—the veterans—stared after him, maybe recognizing the death march for what it was. Maybe getting a preview of their own futures.

When Martin arrived at Jorge's office, he found the door open and Jorge behind his desk, his slightly round features framed by a pair of reading glasses. The Stars' manager looked up from a dog-eared paperback and gestured at the chair in front of his desk. He did not smile, and his dark eyes were unreadable. He looked like a guy about to drop the ax.

Martin sat and, almost by reflex, mounted his defense. "Look, Skip, I know my average is in the toilet, but I'm squaring up some pitches, and they're gonna start falling in." That was bullshit. He was batting .185, and the two balls he'd made contact with in today's game had resulted in little league-strength grounders to the shortstop.

Jorge took in a deep breath and sat back in his chair.

Martin continued his plea before his manager could rebut. "I haven't had a passed ball since I've been here, and I helped Maldonado with his curveball." Here, Martin stood on firmer ground. He remained an able catcher behind the dish, and he called a good game. He also had spotted something in Teoscar Maldonado's delivery—

the kid hurried his motion on his curve and was apt to spike the pitch—and corrected it. The next game, Maldonado struck out eight.

"You're a good catcher," Jorge conceded, finally speaking. His voice was baritone and a little rough around the edges. The kind of voice you could imagine shouting at you, though Jorge never did. "The kids listen to you, and you know what you're talking about."

"Yeah, but. Right?" Martin said and collapsed back in his chair.

"I know you think I'm about to cut you," Jorge began. "Under normal circumstances, I don't have room on this roster for a player in your...condition."

"Normal circumstances? Wait, you're not cutting me?" Martin said. The overwhelming relief almost blunted the knife-shaped word "condition."

"No, I need a catcher with experience who can be patient with a young pitcher. Think that might be you?"

Martin seized on the opportunity like a starving man presented with a crust of bread. "Yeah. Of course. Whatever you need. We got a prospect coming in?"

"Yeah. Just signed him a few weeks ago," Jorge said. "A special case."

"Tell me about him," Martin said. "Where's he from, what's he throw, what's his problem?" This wasn't the first time he'd been asked to take a young pitcher under his wing. Veteran catchers were often assigned to rookie pitchers as part chaperone, part Jedi Master. Catchers were students of the game. They knew how to work an umpire, when you were supposed to throw at a guy who showboated on a homer, as well as the nuts and bolts of pitching. Aging catchers who couldn't bat their weight stuck around in the big leagues for precisely this reason. Well, most of them.

"His name is Andrei Dinescu," Jorge said.

Martin waited for more. When it didn't come, he filled the uncomfortable silence himself. "Okay, that's a new one on me. Where's he from?"

"Moldova."

"I, uh, didn't realize they had organized baseball there," Martin said. In fact, all he knew about Moldova was that it might be next to Romania.

"They don't," Jorge said. The Stars' manager wasn't exactly a loquacious man, but this was ridiculous.

"Give me something, Skip," Martin said. "If I'm gonna help the kid, I need to know something about him."

"I know you do, but it's best you just meet him, work a few bullpens, then make your own evaluation."

"Uh, all right," Martin said, sensing he wasn't going to get anything else. "When does he get here?"

"He's coming in on the red eye. He'll be at the park tomorrow afternoon," Jorge said. "I want you to catch a bullpen with him as soon as he gets here."

Martin weighed whether to ask more questions, but the way Jorge stared at him, serious and unrelenting, made him reconsider. He'd just received a stay of execution, another shot to play baseball for a living...even if only to serve as a glorified chaperone for some bonus baby they'd dug up in Eastern Europe, of all fucking places. "Sounds good. I'll introduce myself when he arrives. He speak English?"

Jorge nodded. "He does, but he doesn't talk much."

Martin got up. "All right, then I'll get out of your hair."

Jorge nodded and waved Martin out of his office. As he turned to go, Martin caught a peek at the book his manager was reading. He couldn't imagine why Jorge Vasquez would be reading the *Old Farmer's Almanac*.

May 11th

The Stars played at Riley Field in West Sacramento, California. It was a relatively new park and fairly expansive as Triple-A stadiums went. Still, every time Martin pulled into the parking lot in his Corvette—one of the few remnants of his major-league lifestyle—all he could see was how much smaller it was than a big-league field. On a good day, Riley Field held 14,000 fans, which seemed like a lot unless you've played in front of 50,000.

Today, Martin arrived feeling better than he had in weeks. His knees still hurt, his back still ached, and a pile of unpaid bills still sat unopened on his kitchen counter, but at least he had something resembling a purpose. If this new prospect turned out to be the real deal, and if he could help the kid's development, there might be a trip back to the majors in his future, or, dare he hope, a coaching position after he retired.

Martin made his way to the locker room and strapped on his gear. Most of the other players were already on the field, taking batting practice, working on defensive plays, and shagging flies. Geared up, Martin headed for the bullpens under the batter's eye in center field. He shouted hellos to his teammates and nodded at Jorge, who was watching Justin Bars take batting practice. Justin was destroying baseballs with wild abandon. As he crossed the field, Martin watched one poor Rawlings sail over the bleachers in right field and out of the park, a distance of well over 450 feet.

The bullpen at Riley Field was enclosed, a long concrete rectangle separated into two pitching lanes by netting. It always felt like pitching in a subway tunnel, and the ball popping the mitt sounded like a gunshot. When Martin showed up for his first bullpen session with Andrei Dinescu, it was quiet as a crypt. Generally, at least one—and usually two—of the Stars' young hurlers were getting in a side session and working on mechanics with pitching coach Julian Tate. Tate—who they all called Tater—was a stocky black man in his early sixties with a still-muscular physique, a bald head, and a goatee that surrounded his mouth in a halo of white. He'd never played in the big leagues, but he'd been a career minor leaguer, and what he couldn't do with his own arm, he excelled in showing more talented folks how to do with theirs.

Tater sat on the long, slatted bench that lined the bullpen wall, his starter's jacket on. On the other end of the bench, about as far from Tater as possible, sat the mysterious Andrei Dinescu. As Martin entered the pen, Tater shot to his feet and stalked over, scowling. "Where the fuck have you been, man?"

"Hey, hey," Martin said. "Skip said be here at two p.m. I just had to put my gear on." He fished his phone from his back pocket. The time showed 2:01. He showed it to

Tater.

The Stars' pitching coach seemed to calm a little. "Sorry, Wags, I just . . ." He glanced back at the huddled shape at the other end of the pen. Andrei Dinescu sat hunched over, staring at the ground. His cap sat on the bench beside him, and a lot of coal-black hair obscured the kid's face. He wore a uniform, but the Stars' gray hung on him like it was two sizes too big.

"You what?" Martin said. "You warm him up?"

Tater shook his head. "That's your job. I'm just supposed to watch, use the radar gun."

"What do you mean you're *just* gonna watch?" Martin said, confused. "You're the pitching coach, for Christ's sake."

"I'm gonna do what Skip told me to do." There was an angry bite in the man's words, but beneath that, something else. He was spooked.

"Okay, fine, did you at least talk to the kid?" Martin asked. "Find out how he's feeling."

"I told you, man. I'm only supposed to fuckin' watch," Tater said between clenched teeth.

"Jesus, Tater," Martin snapped, finally reaching his bullshit quota in the conversation. "Why are you acting so goddamn weird?"

Tater took a step back. "I'm…I'm just trying to do my job. Trying to do what they tell me."

Martin instantly felt like an asshole, and he patted Tater on the shoulder. "It's cool, man. I'm sorry for snapping. Knees hurting like a motherfucker today." No lie there. "I'll go meet the kid, and then we'll throw a little. Sound good?"

Tater blew out a long breath, like he'd been holding it in for a while. "Yeah, good. I'll get the radar gun and get set up." He vacated the pen and left Martin alone with the Stars' newest player.

Martin walked down the candy-green artificial turf lane toward the bench. As he approached, Andrei Dinescu did not look up. In fact, he didn't move until Martin stood right in front of him; then he just kind of flinched back, as if the presence of another person repelled him.

"Hey, kid," Martin said.

Finally, Andrei peered up through a tangle of black hair. His eyes were large and dark and surrounded by bloodshot whites. The tip of his nose peeked through the curtain of hair as well—long, thin, almost beaklike. Beneath that, full lips turned slightly down, and a scrubby goatee on his chin, the kind kids grew when they couldn't grow real beards. Andrei's lips moved, but no words came.

"You wanna stand up and shake my hand?" Martin said, simultaneously creeped out and a little insulted by the Moldovan import lurking in his bullpen.

Andrei rose from the bench with a rustle of fabric and pushed his hair away from his face with one hand. Martin could now see more of the boy's features. They were coarse, though not ugly; the cheekbones, high and sharp, gave him a gaunt appearance. His eyebrows were one solid black line over his eyes. What shocked Martin was the kid's size. He couldn't be more than five-foot-eight and 140 pounds.

Martin stuck out his hand. "I'm Martin Wagner, your

catcher. Most folks call me Wags."

Andrei reached out gingerly and took Martin's hand in a surprisingly strong grip. "Pleased to meet you," he said softly, his Eastern European accent giving the words a slightly ominous lilt. Martin could almost hear the nicknames. *Count Dinescu* sprang instantly to mind.

"Okay, let's talk about a few things." Martin sat on the bullpen bench and patted the wood beside him.

Andrei sat down about a foot away, his entire demeanor one of almost complete exhaustion. Jorge said the kid came in on the red eye, so maybe his odd behavior was only due to a lack of sleep and the awkwardness of being the new guy in a new country. If Martin was honest, the kid made him a little uneasy, though he didn't understand why. He certainly wasn't physically imposing.

"So, you're, uh, from Moldova, huh?" Martin said, thinking a little small talk might break the ice.

Andrei nodded.

"Whereabouts?" Martin asked as if he knew fuck-all about the geography of an Eastern European country he doubted he could find on a map.

"Small village. It…has no name."

"Did you play baseball there?" Martin asked.

Andrei shook his head, and his eyes took on a strange, haunted look.

"Where did you learn to play then?"

"There was a school," Andrei said.

"Like a high school? College? Did you play organized ball there?"

"No, a school for . . . people like me."

"People like you, huh?" What did the kid mean by that? Andrei was as forthcoming about his origins as Jorge had been. Fine. Baseball, then. "Okay, let's get down to brass tacks. What do you throw?"

Andrei blinked at him uncomprehendingly.

"You're a pitcher, right? What kind of pitches do you throw?"

Andrei said nothing for a moment, then something penetrated the exhausted murk in his eyes, and a spark of recognition flared. "Fastball."

"Four-seam? Two-seam?"

Again, the bewildered blink.

Martin sighed, reached into the duffel at his feet, and pulled out a baseball. He handed it to Andrei. "When you throw a fastball, how do you hold it? Show me."

Andrei took the ball and put his index and middle fingers across the seams in a passable four-seam fastball grip.

"Okay, good. What about a breaking pitch?"

No blink this time, just an I-have-no-fucking-idea-what-you-said stare.

Martin made a dipping motion with his hand. "You know, a breaking pitch. A curveball. A slider." It was like explaining baseball to someone who'd seen it on TV once. How the fuck did this kid get drafted? The whole situation reeked of weird. Prospects didn't come unheralded in the middle of the night from parts of former Eastern Bloc countries that wouldn't know baseball from baklava.

"I throw a curveball," Andrei said, and this time he cupped the ball in a C made by his thumb and forefinger. It looked to Martin like a 12-6 curveball grip.

The bullpen door opened, and Tater entered carrying the radar gun. He looked harried and pissed off. "You ain't throwing yet?"

"I need to know *what* he throws first, Tater," Martin said. He resisted adding, *Like his fucking pitching coach should.* "Four-seam fastball and a twelve-to-six curveball." Two pitches weren't enough for a starting pitcher unless those pitches were exceptional. Starters needed at least a change-up or a two-seam fastball to mix in to keep hitters from sitting fast or slow. He gave Andrei another appraising look, and the word *exceptional* was not one he'd use to describe anything about the kid. Creepy? Yes. Exceptional? No.

"Fine, let's get started," Tater replied as he posted up near the plate at the other end of the pen.

"Andrei, we're gonna throw a few," Martin said. "That okay?"

Andrei nodded and picked up his glove from where it sat beside him. It looked brand new, stiff, and not broken in. He trudged toward the pitching rubber and stood listlessly atop it.

Martin trotted down to the other end of the pen, put on his mask, and squatted behind the dish. "We'll go over signs later," he called out. "For now, I'll just call out what I want you to throw."

Andrei nodded.

"Give me the heater," Martin said and held his glove up. Even from sixty feet, six inches away, Martin could see that slow, bewildered blink. *Jesus fucking Christ.* "Throw a fastball."

Andrei brought the ball and glove together at his

waist, raised them slowly over his head, took a step, and threw. The ball came out in a three-quarters arm slot and didn't look half bad, but when the ball hit the mitt, the mystery behind Andrei Dinescu's sudden appearance in a Stars' uniform only thickened.

Martin didn't need Tater to tell him the pitch hadn't broken eighty, but the pitching coach called out, "Seventy-two."

"Hey, Andrei," Martin called out. "Not your curveball. I want your fastball."

"That is a fastball," Andrei said, hanging his head, his black hair curtaining his face again.

"Oh, okay . . ." Martin said. He glanced back at Tater and mouthed, *What the fuck?*

The Stars' pitching coach wouldn't meet Martin's gaze.

Martin threw the ball back. Andrei caught it somewhat clumsily. He didn't just sound like someone who had never seen the game played; he looked like it, too.

"Okay, uh, throw some more fastballs then," Martin said.

Andrei threw twenty-four more pitches. Not one of them broke seventy-five. His control was good, and he threw strikes, but a seventy-five-mile-per-hour fastball, even in the minor leagues, was laughable. The average velocity for the old number one in Triple-A clocked in at least ninety-two or ninety-three. In the bigs, it was more like ninety-five. It didn't make any goddamn sense.

Martin got up after the last pitch. "We're done here," he said to Tater and jogged over to Andrei. The Stars' pitching coach vacated the bullpen like his ass was on fire.

Andrei held out the ball as Martin neared. "I am tired. I will throw faster soon."

Martin accepted the ball, a mix of sympathy and apprehension churning in his mind. "Hey, you just got in. Travel can knock the shit out of you, I know. Get some rest, and we'll work on some stuff in your next bullpen." *Like somehow finding you an extra twenty miles-per-hour on your heater.*

Andrei nodded and trudged off toward the bullpen door, leaving Martin holding the ball. He should head out and take batting practice. He was supposed to catch tonight, and he'd like to put the bat on the ball with authority for once, but as he left the bullpen, his feet carried him to Jorge Vasquez's office.

Jorge was poring over the lineup card when Martin entered his office. He knocked on the open door, and Jorge looked up briefly and pointed to the chair in front of his desk.

Martin sat down. "I had my first bullpen with Dinescu."

"I know. Tater told me."

"Okay, then, can you tell *me* why the organization is hot on a kid who can't throw harder than a beer-league softball pitcher and doesn't appear to have played a single day of organized ball in his life?"

"I can't," Jorge said, sitting back in his chair. Inscrutable.

"Can't or won't?"

"Which will help you do your job?"

Thin ice creaked beneath Martin, but he still found enough stupid to press on. "Look, I want to help the team, but give me something."

Jorge looked down at the lineup card. "When's his next bullpen?"

"Schedule says five days."

"He'll be better then."

"*How* will he be better?"

"I think you should go get some batting practice," Jorge said, ignoring the question. "I'm hitting you eighth tonight."

"Fine. Sure," Martin said, realizing he'd reached the end of whatever rope Jorge was inclined to give him. He got up, his knees popping like pistol shots. They started to ache on his way to the locker room, and if he didn't get the Percocet on board soon, he wouldn't be able to walk, let alone squat behind the plate for tonight's game. The brief glimmer of hope he'd felt when he pulled into the parking lot of Riley Field had disappeared, swallowed by his old friends: doubt and pain.

May 16th

Martin served as the backup catcher for the Stars. The starter, a kid from Missouri named Tanner Shreve, was built like the proverbial brick shithouse, about as bright, and carried a mean streak a mile wide. He could hit a ton but was a complete disaster behind the plate and a real pain in the ass in the locker room. If he made it to the show, he might catch on as a slow-moving, bad-fielding first baseman or, more likely, a designated hitter. The Giants had come to this realization, and Shreve had been playing more first base of late for the Stars. Since they didn't have other high-level catching prospects, Martin picked up the slack.

Between his first bullpen session with Andrei and his next, Martin played in four of the Stars' six home games, and his knees and body were suffering for it. The worst day had been when he caught another highly touted pitching prospect, Hector Morales, who threw enough fifty-seven-foot curveballs to keep Martin diving like a soccer goalie to prevent wild pitches. During those four games, though, through luck or divine intervention, Martin managed five hits, including a homer, raising his average above .200, the oft-cited Mendoza line, for the first time all season.

Bruised and battered, Martin then traveled with the team to Tacoma to play the Mountaineers on their own turf. He looked for Andrei on the bus but didn't find him. In fact, the rookie was MIA until Martin showed up at the park in Tacoma, and Jorge informed him the Moldovan prospect would be ready for his side session at 2:00 p.m.

The visitor bullpen in Tacoma was open air and next to the field. That way, fans could observe and, if the mood took them, jeer at opposing pitchers while they warmed up. Martin found a completely different Andrei Dinescu waiting for him. For one, he stood on the mound, wind-milling his arms and warming up. Two, he'd pulled his hair back in a ponytail and wore a Stars cap. He looked more awake, livelier, and if put to it, Martin might even say the kid seemed to fill out his uniform a little better. They'd probably just found one that fit.

"You're looking better," Martin said.

"I feel better," Andrei said, his voice clearer, brighter, and he actually met Martin's gaze. For lack of a better word, the kid seemed more *normal.*

"You ready to get some work in?"

Andrei nodded. The gesture bordered on enthusiasm.

"Cool. Let's do it." Martin glanced over at the second mound and pitching lane. Tater was working with Hector Morales, going over his curveball grip. Both stole glances at Martin and Andrei. Hector looked curious, but Tater still wore that slightly pissed, slightly freaked-out expression. The Mountaineers' bullpen had an internal radar gun, and a screen on the back wall behind the pitcher showed the pitch speed. Martin wouldn't need Tater to hold the gun, not that the Stars' pitching coach seemed inclined to help.

Martin squatted behind the plate, his knees groaning. The Percocet would kick in soon enough. He was up to six a day and starting to get hungry for the little white pills. He pushed that alarming thought out of his head and called out to Andrei, "Let's warm up with some fastballs."

Andrei nodded and grabbed a ball from the bucket next to the mound. He came set, kicked, and threw. The ball hummed through the air and hit Martin's mitt with a satisfying pop. The screen behind Andrei's head flashed 84 MPH. Martin goggled at the number. Andrei had gained ten miles per hour on his heater in a week. "Uh, throw another one like that."

Again, Andrei buzzed in a fastball, this time posting a speed of eighty-six. Still nothing to crow about in professional baseball, but it was a miraculous improvement. He'd seen pitchers get dead arm, a kind of muscle fatigue, and lose three or four miles per hour off their fastballs, but ten?

Martin noticed Tater watching them. The pitching coach jumped every time the ball hit the mitt. After four more pitches, Tater finished with Hector and left. Hector, a good-natured Dominican guy, lingered behind to watch. "You got good control, man," he said to Andrei between one of the pitches.

Andrei stared as if shocked another person had spoken to him. "Thank you," he said shyly.

"Where you been hiding at, man?" Hector continued. "I don't see you in the clubhouse or on the field." Hector's question was unsurprising. Even when pitchers weren't throwing, they were still around, working with the pitching coach or the strength and conditioning coach, or, hell, shooting the shit with their teammates in the dugout or clubhouse. Andrei had been conspicuously absent from all those activities. It felt like they were hiding him.

Martin watched Andrei tense, as if the question caused him physical pain. "I don't speak...good English."

Bullshit and a cry for help if Martin ever heard one. Before Hector could say anything else, he pointed to the Dominican pitcher. "Hey, Morales, Tater show you how to throw a curveball that actually reaches the plate?"

Hector looked over at him, and his broad face split into a grin. "Fuck you, Wags," he said. "I'll show you in my next start."

"Good, because I'm an old man, and chasing your wild pitches is gonna give me a fucking heart attack." Wags threw the ball back to Andrei.

"No way. You catch everything, man," Hector said, laughing.

"I appreciate the vote of confidence, but I need to work with Andrei. Go catch a shower or something and stop distracting him," Martin said.

"Yeah, okay. Sorry, Wags," Hector said and got up. He threw a puzzled glance at Andrei, then left the bullpen.

"You know, you're gonna have to talk to someone other than me and Skip at some point," Martin said to Andrei. "The guys are gonna think you're a prima donna or something."

"They said...they said I should not talk to anyone but you," Andrei replied.

"Who's they?" Martin asked. "Skip? Tater?"

Andrei stared at him, unblinking, turning the ball over and over in his hand. "I just want to play. They said..." He stopped himself, shaking his head as if to ward off the thought.

Martin got up and approached him. "You can talk to me, kid. I promise."

Andrei opened his mouth, and his eyes took on a desperate, pleading look. *Here it comes,* Martin thought. *The fucked-up truth.* Instead, Andrei closed his mouth and shook his head.

Martin sighed and walked back to the plate. "Let's see

that curveball."

Turned out Andrei's curveball was a good one, with tight spin and excellent drop. It might even be good enough to make his fastball play in the minors. When he got back to the clubhouse, Martin found Jorge waiting by his locker. The rest of the team was changing into their uniforms and getting ready for the game. Martin was riding the bench tonight. Tanner Shreve would be handling the catcher's duties.

"What's up, Skip?" Martin asked and began removing his gear.

"How'd he do?" Jorge crossed his arms over his broad chest.

Martin sat on his stool and shook his head. "You know, it's weird you're asking me when I feel like you already know."

Jorge's eyes narrowed, and the ghost of a smile flickered across his lips. "He threw harder, didn't he?"

"His fastball topped out at eighty-six," Martin admitted.

"That's an improvement."

"Borderline miraculous," Martin said and stripped off his uniform. He had a clean one hanging in the locker. He'd change into it before game time so he could sit in the dugout with his teammates. With Shreve catching, there was a not-insignificant chance Martin would get called into the game as a defensive replacement if the Stars had a late lead.

"I told you he'd get better." This time Jorge did smile, smugly.

"Sure, better, but you gonna tell me a mid-eighties fastball and a halfway-decent curve warrant whatever the fuck is going on here?" Martin's relief at a possible second chance had mostly evaporated. He didn't like being kept in the dark.

Jorge shrugged. "Greg Maddux didn't throw much harder than that."

"Oh, so the kid's a Hall-of-Famer now?" Martin laughed.

"Look, Wags, I know this is a strange assignment. I'm sorry for that, but if you don't think you can handle the job, there are a dozen aging catchers out there who'd catch bullets if I offered them a contract."

Martin's mouth fell open at the bluntness of the threat. "I'm not saying I can't do the job," he said, almost whispering.

"Good," Jorge said. "Keep at it. Andrei will surprise you."

"You gonna put him in a game soon?" Martin asked, and instantly regretted it.

Jorge answered with a question of his own. "What is today?"

"Sunday, May sixteenth," Martin said.

"We're back home on the twenty-first. Maybe a relief appearance on the homestand. In the meantime, keep working his bullpens." Jorge then turned and headed toward the managerial offices, leaving Martin to wonder what would happen on the 21st.

When the game started, Martin watched the action on the field with little interest, paying attention out of habit. He couldn't pull his mind away from his bullpen with Andrei or the increasingly bizarre conversations with his manager.

What he wanted was someone to talk to, someone to lay all this weird shit on who might give him some perspective. He couldn't talk to his teammates. They'd have as many questions as he did. Tater seemed to know something, but the man's attitude blared, *Stay the fuck away from me*. No help there.

Then Martin spied Stephanie Olsen, the Stars' strength and conditioning coach, giving John Marconi, the Stars' starting pitcher, a quick massage on his pitching arm between innings.

Stephanie was an athletic woman, on the short side with frizzy reddish-blonde hair and skin so pale she was practically translucent. She was funny, smart, and she and Martin had hooked up a few times after drinks. Two adults nursing recent failed relationships and taking a bit of comfort in each other. They told each other the same bullshit, that neither of them was looking for anything serious. Martin almost believed it, but the last time had been different. It wasn't just fooling around; he'd felt something deeper. He thought she might have felt it, too, but she'd been distant ever since, and he hadn't pressed the issue.

He waited for Stephanie to finish with Marconi, then

followed her down the tunnel into the gym attached to the visitors' locker room. It was thankfully empty. "Hey, Steph," he called out. No one, not even the S&C coach, escaped the inevitable baseball name-shortening tradition.

She turned and smiled. Martin felt a little flutter in his stomach at that smile, like a schoolboy the prettiest girl in class has just noticed and spoken to for the first time. "What's up, Wags? How're the knees?"

"Uh, fine, you know. Ice and Percocet for the win."

Her face took on a serious expression, one she probably used to cajole lazy ballplayers into showing up for their workouts. "I know you do what you have to, but be careful with that stuff, will ya?"

"Hey, uh, you wanna grab a drink after the game?" he said, flatly ignoring her concern. She wasn't wrong. He just had more looming issues than his nascent pill addiction.

Something flickered across her eyes, something that made him think, *Uh oh.* "Um, you know, Wags, I started seeing someone."

Martin hadn't expected that, and even though his goal hadn't been anything more than a conversation, and even though they'd agreed it was nothing serious, he couldn't deny he had hoped their relationship would have become something more than friendship with occasional, impersonal sex. "Oh, that's awesome," he said, trying—and failing miserably—to hide his hurt feelings behind feigned enthusiasm.

"I'm sorry," Steph said, sounding like she meant it. That made Martin feel worse somehow.

"Jesus, this is gonna sound bad now, but I really just want to talk," Martin said.

"Okay," Steph replied warily. "What about?"

"The new kid, Andrei Dinescu. They stuck me with him, and…" He glanced around the little gym. "Have you worked with him yet?" Every player on the team worked with Steph in some fashion. It was Steph's job to make sure they maintained fitness programs that kept them strong and injury-free.

"Yeah, I have. A handful of times," Steph said. That wariness remained, but Martin sensed it no longer had anything to do with him. "Then Skip said the kid didn't need my services anymore."

That was more than strange; it was downright bizarre. "You've seen something?"

"Have *you* seen something?" she asked back.

"Look, this is why I wanted to talk. Not here, though. Will you have a drink with me after the game?"

Steph's eyes roved around the room, probably to make sure they were alone, then she nodded, "Okay, yeah, but this shit stays between us. I got a real fucked-up feeling we're entering lose-your-job territory."

He was touched that she trusted him enough to take that risk. It softened the blow that they'd never be more than friends. He realized now, far too late, that he *had* wanted more out of their little fling. That ship had apparently sailed. "Great. I'll meet you in the parking lot at ten."

"Fine. Now get back into the dugout before someone sees us talking," she said, putting a finger in the middle of his chest. "And find something other than Percocet for your knees."

"Sure thing, Coach. Just as soon as those robot legs I ordered from Amazon show up," he said as he turned to go.

Her laughter, the same laughter they'd shared over drinks and later in bed, made everything hurt a little more.

The Stars were behind for most of the game, trailing by two runs until the top of the eighth, when Justin Bars hit a 3–1 hanging slider into orbit with two men on. That gave the Stars a one-run lead going into the bottom of the inning, and, as Martin suspected, he was put in to replace Tanner Shreve, who already had two passed balls under his belt for the night.

None too pleased to be taken out, Shreve let Jorge know when the skipper gave him the news. "It's bullshit, Skip," he complained, his voice surprisingly high and whiny for a linebacker-sized catcher. "They should have given Marconi a wild pitch on those two. I couldn't have blocked 'em."

This was bullshit of the highest order. Both pitches were back-foot sliders any catcher with the minimum agility of a Mack truck could have blocked. Jorge wasted no time in pointing this out loudly while the rest of the team looked on. The color drained from Shreve's face, and he sat down with a thump, pouting like a 265-pound toddler.

"Wags, you're in," Jorge called out, and Martin strapped

on the gear.

The Stars' closer was another guy destined for better things. Oliver Yang was a tall, reedy twenty-year-old with a mop of raggedy brown hair that always seemed to escape his cap in clumps. He looked about as athletic as the poor kid who gets chosen last for sports in PE. But the Almighty had reached down and touched Oliver's right arm, imbuing it with an upper nineties fastball with enough movement to confound even the league's best hitters. He'd get the call up soon.

Yang struck out the side in the bottom of the eighth on twelve pitches, and Jorge left him in for the ninth, where he struck out another two batters. The only contact made was a weak grounder along the first base line. An easy out that secured a Stars victory.

Martin celebrated with his teammates on the field, congratulating Yang for a great save, then skipped the spread laid out in the visitors' locker room, a kingly feast provided by Taco Bell. The shitty food in the minors served as yet another reminder of how far Martin had fallen.

Steph was waiting for him when Martin made it to the parking lot. She looked good in her street clothes. Nothing fancy, just jeans and a tank top, but they showed off her curves and the lean muscles in her arms and shoulders. "Where's your mid-life-crisis car, champ?" she asked with a wry smile. She gave him no end of shit about his Corvette.

Martin laughed. "I don't take the 'Vette on road trips. I don't like to flaunt my staggering success, you know?" He went for cute and sarcastic and overshot straight into bitterness. Steph was nice enough not to say anything.

They called an Uber, and because Martin didn't know Tacoma well, he chose the closest spot, one of those shit-all-over-the-wall sports bars in the vein of TGI Fridays. This one was an off-brand joint called Coasters that promised bottomless beer pitchers and eight big-screen TVs.

Steph didn't seem to mind the low-rent locale. They both knew the score financially. He was a washed-up form-er big-leaguer with debt up to his eyeballs, and she was the strength-and-conditioning coach for a minor-league baseball team, a gig that paid a skosh more than a high school PE teacher.

They grabbed a booth near the back of the restaurant, ordered a pitcher of beer, then attempted small talk for a bit. Their former intimacy and the hard line recently drawn in their relationship sand made things increasingly awkward. Martin gave up before he finished his first beer and launched into why he'd asked Steph here in the first place.

"I've done two bullpen sessions with Dinescu," Martin said.

Steph sipped her beer and peered over the glass at him. "You first. Tell me what happened."

"Well, you've seen the kid," he said. "He makes Yang look like fucking Hercules. Not much physique or any-thing I'd call athletic. He barely registered on the radar gun in our first side session. I'm talking mid-seventies."

"Right," she said. "And the second one?" That ques-tion came across loaded. He had a feeling she knew exactly what that second bullpen had been like.

"Today, the kid comes in, looks rested, and I shit you not, he looks *bigger*," Martin said.

"Threw harder too, right?" Steph said.

"Ten miles per hour harder," Martin said. "Who the fuck does that?"

"Nobody I know," she said and sighed. "Okay, I guess you showed me yours."

He chuckled and blushed. Their badinage before she'd made the announcement in the gym had been laced with innuendo. He knew it didn't mean anything, but even if they couldn't be lovers, he liked hanging out with her.

"Jorge introduced me to him maybe a day after he came in from wherever they found him," Steph began. "Never heard of him, and no one warned me I needed to come up with a program for a new pitcher."

Martin nodded. "I got a little more warning than that, but Skip wouldn't tell me shit other than where he came from and that I was his babysitter."

She took a pull from her beer, not a sip this time, and continued. "Well, he comes by with the kid in tow and tells me to work with him, right then and there." She shook her head. "Like, what the fuck am I supposed to do? Which I said, though in more professional terminology. Skip tells me just work him out, then plops down on one of the bench presses to watch."

Martin blinked. "That is really fucking weird."

"Right?" Steph said. "So, I put Dinescu through a basic full-body routine. Nothing strenuous, just trying to figure out if he had any trouble spots we might work on, see what kind of flexibility he had, get some baseline maximums, that kind of stuff."

"And?" Martin prodded, although he had a pretty good idea.

Before Steph could continue, the waiter, a good-looking kid with the green Coaster's uniform decked out in buttons and pins, sidled up to their table. "You folks want another pitcher, something to eat?"

Martin threw the server an irritated glare, but to his surprise, Steph spoke up. "Yeah, bring us the loaded nachos and another pitcher."

"You got it." The server moved off to place their order.

"What?" Steph said, catching Martin looking at her appraisingly. "I'm hungry, and I've never seen *you* turn down food."

If she was eating with him, that meant she was comfortable, and if she was comfortable... Martin stopped himself. Wishful thinking. "You're right; I have never turned down nachos in my entire life," he said with a short laugh. "You were talking about Andrei."

"Right. So the kid is scrawny, and that's being polite," she said. "He was weak as a kitten for that first workout. He could barely lift more than the bar on most exercises. The entire time I'm working him out, Skip is sitting there, writing stuff down in a little notebook."

"He ever done that with any other rookies?" Martin asked.

"Nope. I just give him updates on their progress."

"Let me guess. Ol' Andrei was a changed man on

your second workout, right?"

She made a finger gun at him. "He comes in with Skip again and looks more alert...more alive, for lack of a better word. He's stronger, too. Like a lot stronger. Nothing earth-shattering, but something approximating the output of a professional athlete."

"When was that?" Martin asked.

"Four days ago," she said. "He had another session today, I guess after his bullpen with you."

Martin leaned forward. "Yeah, and how did that go?"

"Look, I've seen players on the juice," she said. "When I got into baseball, it was everywhere. I know what that looks like."

"What happened today?"

"Skip brings him in, and this time the kid actually takes off his uniform shirt, and he's got a tank top underneath. Martin, the muscles I saw on that kid's frame weren't fucking there a week ago. I'd stake my life on it."

"You don't think it's steroids then?" he said. He actually had no experience with anabolics himself, though it had been rampant when he'd come into the league. Part of him wished he had done a cycle or two to see if it would have meant a few more homers, a few more doubles, but he'd wanted to make it on his own natural talent. Turned out he didn't have enough of that.

"No way," she said. "To go from beanpole to beach body in under two weeks? Not to mention, the kid put up one eighty-five on the bench press today in reps of ten when he could barely get the bar off his chest before."

"What then?" Martin said.

Their nachos and beer arrived before Steph could answer, and they both filled their mugs, then stared at the food like it was a plate of toxic waste. Seemed they'd both lost their appetites.

"I don't know what," Steph said. "But I don't see the kid in the locker room, I don't see him in the dugout, he's not on the travel bus, and Jorge is acting like he's in the witness protection program."

"You think that could be it, maybe?" Martin asked. The idea had actually occurred to him. "Maybe he's got some kind of trouble back home, and they're keeping a close eye on him because of it."

She shook her head. "No, that doesn't feel right." She paused, took a big gulp of beer, and then looked Martin in the eyes. "I'll tell you what it feels like. It *feels* like an experiment or something. All the notes Jorge took during our workout, the secrecy. I'm getting serious lab-rat vibes."

Martin remembered Jorge asking for pitch speeds and having Tater there to record them. That hadn't stuck out because it was standard baseball shit, but added to Steph's experience… "What's the experiment?"

She raised her eyebrows. "They gonna put him in a game soon?"

"Next homestand," Martin said.

"There you go. Whatever is going on with this kid, they think it might help win ballgames. I mean, come on. How many times has the big club experimented with guys in the minors? Sending them down so they can learn a new position or a new pitch."

He took in a breath and grimaced. "And I get a front

row seat to the show."

She raised her beer mug. "Better you than me."

"You're an asshole," he said and clinked her glass. "Will you keep me updated on anything that goes on with Andrei in the gym?"

"I will." She looked away for a moment, then reached across the table and took his hand. The warmth of her touch was electric, and it summoned up thoughts he definitely should not be thinking. "Be careful, Wags. I got a bad feeling about this."

He smiled and pulled his hand away, maybe too quickly by the look on her face. "I'll be fine," he said, then cast around for the waiter so he could get their bill. He desperately wanted to get out of there. Steph had spooked him, and, more than that, the beer buzz had laid bare his feelings for her.

He flagged down the waiter, paid the bill, and Steph both surprised and disappointed him by calling her own Uber. He laughed it off, but watching her drive away in the ubiquitous blue Prius felt like the world's shittiest goodbye.

)ᗡᗞ🌑🌒🌘(

The Stars, led by the thunderous bat of Justin Bars, took three of four games from the Mountaineers. He hit four homers and a pair of doubles in the series, and Martin wouldn't be surprised if Justin got the call-up when they returned to Sacramento.

Martin started one of the four games, where he picked up two hits and a couple RBIs. He also came in as a defensive replacement in two other games to make sure the Stars could hold on to slim leads. All that playing, as welcome as it was, turned his knees into twin motes of screaming agony. Ice helped, Percocet helped more, and the ounce of weed he scored from Teoscar Maldonado didn't hurt either. The Dominican pitcher offered it in gratitude for Martin helping him with his changeup. He got dangerously high once, but he had to admit it took the edge off the pain.

Martin didn't see Andrei again. He popped into the gym once to ask if Steph had. Her demeanor was a little stiff after their strange encounter the other night, but he believed her when she said Andrei hadn't been in to work out. Martin briefly considered asking Jorge, but the last conversation he'd had with the manager had been decidedly unpleasant. He decided he'd wait and see what happened.

They arrived back in Sacramento on the 20th at about four in the afternoon. No game that night, so the players had the rest of the day to themselves. Martin had no interest in carousing with his younger teammates, so he went back to his apartment to smoke what remained of Maldonado's weed.

There was a notice from Julie's attorney waiting for him on the floor when he opened the door. Guess she'd let him slide as far as she could. He sighed, picked it up, and threw it on the counter next to bills and credit card offers. His apartment was billed as a one bedroom, but the closet-sized room they'd squeezed into the sumptuous

500 square feet hardly qualified.

He rolled a joint, badly—he'd never learned the trick—poured himself a couple fingers of whiskey, and retreated into his bedroom. He turned on the sixty-inch TV mounted on the wall, a trophy from better days, flipped around until he found a mindless cooking show, and proceeded to get righteously stoned.

At some point, he passed out. When he woke, the sun streamed through the window, his head felt like someone had shoved it full of cotton and then wailed on it with a baseball bat, and his phone informed him it was somehow, inexplicably, 1:00 p.m. on May 21st. He sat up, managed not to vomit, and tried to come to terms with the fact he had to play baseball in six short hours.

May 21st

Aleve, Percocet, Visine, and two bottles of Perrier got Martin into something resembling playing shape by the time he arrived at the field. He went straight to his locker, sat on the stool, and took in deep gulps of air. The other guys were getting dressed and shooting the shit. Most paid him no mind, but Tanner Shreve saw him from across the room and smirked.

Martin didn't like that smirk. That smirk said trouble. That smirk said I'm gonna start shit, and that's exactly what Shreve did. The big catcher got up—he'd just come from the showers and wore only a towel around his waist—a ponderous, meaty mountain of a kid, as agile as a dump truck and mean as a three-legged pit bull.

Shreve sauntered across the locker room, his smirk growing into a malicious smile. Others noticed his purposeful line toward Martin, and a mixture of concern and excitement bloomed on their faces.

"Hey, old man," Shreve said, putting his foot on a nearby stool and giving Martin a clear view of his dick and balls under his towel. It was a weird flex, especially since the kid didn't have much to brag about in that department. "You know, it's bullshit they keep pulling me out of games for your old ass. What do you think?"

Martin tried not to roll his eyes. If he'd been a little less hungover, he might have noticed the situation festering under his nose for the past week. He'd been so preoccupied with Andrei he hadn't paid attention to much else. Shreve was a mean, stupid, immature asshole, and the fact he'd taken umbrage at being pulled for a defensive replacement wasn't surprising. Martin stood up and looked the Stars' starting catcher in the eyes. He had to look up to do it. "What do I think?" Martin said. "You really want to know?"

The smile flickered on Shreve's face, a momentary surge of doubt all bullies experience when their victims don't just roll over and show their bellies. "Yeah, I would."

The rest of the guys in the locker room had gathered behind them. Some looked downright gleeful at the prospect of a fight. Others wore expressions of disapproval. None of them would interfere, of course. These things had to be worked out in the most toxic, male, bullshit fashion possible.

Martin was both shorter and lighter than Shreve. And, of course, he was fifteen years older, his body a collection of aches, pains, and semi-successful surgeries, all held together by narcotics and stubbornness. In short, if it came to blows, Shreve would kick the shit out of him, but Martin was in a real fuck-it mood. "I think, Tanner, you are bar-fucking-none the worst goddamn catcher I have laid eyes on in professional baseball."

Shreve sucked in a breath—not quite a gasp—and his face reddened. Martin continued. "I also think even if the pitcher was throwing basketballs, you'd commit four passed balls a night and *still* blame it on the pitcher like a giant fucking man-baby."

Shreve's eyes had gone wide and goggling, an expression mirrored on the faces of the guys behind him. That was partly because they all knew Martin was right and partly because they all knew what had to happen now.

Martin had an entire second to take satisfaction in his stunning rebuke, and then Shreve's right fist came up in a blur and smashed into his face. Martin reeled back against his locker, fighting for balance, stars bursting across his vision, blood trickling down his cheek from where one of Shreve's knuckles had cut him above the eye. He tried to regain his balance and fight back, but Shreve steamed forward, ham hock-sized fists flailing.

"Motherfucker! Motherfucker!" the big catcher shouted with each whistling haymaker, like his entire vocabulary had been reduced to one rage-filled word.

Martin got an arm up to protect himself. Shreve's punches weren't accurate, but they landed with such force they battered Martin left and right. He managed to land a jab of his own, bloodying Shreve's nose, but the pale gargantuan didn't seem to notice or care.

The other guys were shouting now, and Martin caught sight of Justin Bars racing toward them. The horrifying idea of Justin suffering some terrible career-ending injury over this shit scared Martin more than getting his face beat in by the poster child for white privilege.

A couple of guys headed Justin off and held him back, likely having the same thought as Martin, while others attempted to pull Shreve away. He violently shrugged them off, catching Teoscar Maldonado on the chin with the point of his shoulder and dropping the pitcher to the floor. He was out cold.

"Get Skip!" someone shouted. It sounded like Tater.

Martin caught another fist in the belly, smashing the air from his lungs and doubling him over. He straightened just in time to catch a clumsy left on the forehead, rocking him back against the locker again. Shreve had a strange look in his eyes. It had gone beyond anger, beyond shame, and had morphed into something uglier. Shreve was enjoying himself.

The big catcher pulled back his right fist for another punch, and then, a heartbeat later, he was pinned against the locker next to Martin, choking for air, Andrei Dinescu's right hand wrapped around his throat. The pitcher was in uniform, his ball cap was on, and his hair was in a neat ponytail behind his head. The muscles on his forearm bunched and writhed as he held immobile a man who outweighed him by a hundred pounds.

Shreve gagged and beat at Andrei's arm. He might as well have been trying to chop down a redwood with a plastic fork. The catcher's face reddened again, not from anger this time.

Andrei's mouth split in a feral sneer, and his teeth, white and straight, were bared. His eyes, like black voids, bored into Shreve's, and Martin felt certain Andrei would kill the Stars' starting catcher.

"Andrei," Martin said, trying to stand up straight. His ribs ached, and he couldn't pull enough breath into his lungs to speak above a whisper. This time, the other players wanted no part of the altercation. They stood motionless, stunned, some with mouths open in dumb shock.

"Andrei," Martin said, louder this time; the pitcher looked at him. Those black eyes were twin pits that sucked the strength from Martin's legs, but he put his hands on Andrei's arm and tried to pull it away. He had about as much success as Shreve, whose own efforts had become feeble and fluttering as he began to lose consciousness.

"*Sângele lui Ailbe*!" came a hoarse shout that cut through the locker room like a gunshot. The syllables were alien, probably more so since they'd come packaged in Jorge's Mexican accent. He followed them up in plain, old English. "Let him go!"

The effect was immediate. Andrei released Shreve, and the catcher collapsed to the floor, sucking in huge, wheezing gulps of air, tears streaming from his bloodshot eyes.

Andrei hung his head and stepped back. His eyes held remorse, but his mouth was still twisted in that ugly sneer.

Martin collapsed on his stool, grabbed a towel from

his locker, and dabbed at the blood running down his cheek.

"I'm...sorry," Andrei said softly.

"Andrei," Jorge said as he approached, flanked by Mike Embrey and Tater. "Go with Mike and cool off."

"Come on, kid," Mike said, regarding Andrei like a man might a particularly vicious dog. Andrei, for his part, simply slunk after the Stars' bench coach, shoulders slumped, eyes on the ground. More whipped mutt than vicious dog.

"Get Shreve and Maldonado to the training room and have Steph look at them," Jorge ordered, and some of the guys moved to help both men from the floor. Maldonado was at least sitting up, but the dazed look in his eyes said he might have a concussion. Shreve got to his feet on his own, though he looked like he might fall over any minute. His nakedness and the angry red marks on his throat almost made Martin feel sorry for him. Almost.

When Shreve and Maldonado left the room, Jorge pulled up a stool next to Martin, his face twisted in an ugly frown. "What the fuck happened, Wags?" he said, his voice laced with anger and disappointment.

"Hey, Skip," Justin Bars said from behind his manager. He had thankfully emerged unscathed from the little row. "Shreve swung first. I saw it." Spurred by Bars, other players echoed the sentiment.

Jorge kept his eyes on Martin but said, "Noted. Don't you have a game to get ready for?" His tone brooked no further discussion on the incident.

Justin opened his mouth to say something else, maybe something like, *Hey, Skip, how does a hundred-and-forty pound nobody from nowhere manhandle a two hundred-and-sixty-five-pound tub of asshole like he's lifting a sack of garbage?* He thought better of it, though, nodded, and retreated to his locker.

"You heard Bars," Martin began. "Shreve took a swing at me. I was trying to protect myself."

"*Why* did he take a swing at you?" Jorge said. His eyes narrowed, and the accusation hung as thick as a fart in an elevator.

Martin pulled the towel away from his head with a hiss. It was stained red. He probably needed stitches. "Because I told him he's the worst fucking catcher ever to squat behind the dish." No point in lying. Everyone had heard him.

To Martin's surprise, Jorge chuckled. "Can't argue with that. Kid's a problem, and not just because he couldn't block a river with a fucking dam."

"I let it get out of hand," Martin said. That was as far into an apology as he would go. "Now, tell me what you said to Andrei. I'm pretty sure you didn't know much Moldovan or Romanian or whatever the fuck that was until a month ago."

Jorge grimaced but did not look away. It was as close to an admittance of how bizarre the situation had become as Martin had seen from his manager. Still, the man steadfastly ignored the question. "I need you to catch tonight."

"Are you kidding me?" Martin said. "I'm fucking bleeding, Skip."

"I was the bench coach for the Houston Astros in 2014," Jorge said. "We were playing the Giants in a three-game series, and you caught the second game."

Martin rolled his eyes. He remembered the game, and he knew where his manager was going with this story.

"Sonny Ishihara caught you with the backswing when he missed Terry Sutter's curveball by about six feet and knocked you on your ass," Jorge continued. Ishihara, a recent import from the Japanese professional baseball league, had a penchant for wild swings. "He knocked you out cold, didn't he?"

Martin rubbed his jaw and nodded. "Yeah, he did."

"And you finished the game."

"Yes, but I shouldn't have," Martin said. He'd been nauseous for days with blurred vision and all the other telltale symptoms of a concussion, but he knew if he went on the Injured List for any length of time, he'd get sent down and maybe stay there. That's what happened to marginal players. He hadn't told anyone, and he'd gutted out the next week of games.

"Probably not, but I'm gonna put Andrei in for a relief appearance, and I want you in there to catch him," Jorge said. "Not to mention, Shreve is gonna take a little trip down to Double-A so he can think about his attitude, and it's gonna take me a day to promote another catcher."

"You're gonna put the kid in after this shit?" Martin said, pitching his voice low. "If you hadn't said those magic words or whatever, I think he might have killed Shreve."

Jorge shook his head. "No. No danger of that. Yet."

"Yet? What the fuck is that supposed to mean?" Martin said.

"It means he's gonna pitch tonight, you're gonna catch him, and that's how it is," Jorge said and stood up. "Plus, the kid likes you."

"How do you figure?" Martin asked.

Jorge shrugged. "He didn't let Shreve beat you to death."

Steph ran Martin through the concussion protocols in the training room. Much to both their surprise, they were negative. He'd always had a hard head. Then she sat him on one of the massage tables, cleaned up the cut above his eye, and closed it with a butterfly bandage. Like most team trainers, she had an EMT license and could deal with minor medical concerns. "You need stitches," she said, frowning.

"Probably, but I gotta play tonight," Martin said and hopped down from the table. He winced when he made contact with the floor. The pain in his head almost let him forget the pain in his knees.

"I hear Andrei almost ripped Shreve's head off," Steph said. "Not that that overgrown fuck-stick didn't deserve it."

"It wasn't that bad, though I wouldn't expect Shreve to be doing much karaoke for a few weeks," Martin replied. "Dinescu is spooky strong, just like you said."

"He's pitching tonight, isn't he?" Steph replied. "That's why you're playing."

Martin said nothing. Not that he needed to.

"Goddamn it, Wags. You should be at the hospital with Shreve and Maldonado. They could call someone up from San Jose in an hour if they needed a catcher. They don't need you."

Her concern touched Martin. "You're right, but I wouldn't want anyone else catching the kid."

"Why?"

"This won't make much sense," Martin said, remembering what Jorge had said about Andrei liking him. "But I think it'd be dangerous for anyone but me."

Steph cocked her head and stared at him. "So, you *do* think he's dangerous?"

"I... I don't know," Martin said lamely. He did know, though. He'd seen the look on Andrei's face while he was strangling Shreve. He'd seen the strength in the kid's body, that wild look in his eyes. The fact Andrei had lost control maybe to protect Martin said he might have some sway with him. Enough sway to keep some seriously bad shit from happening.

"Bullshit," Steph said with a snort. Then she patted him awkwardly on the hand, her eyes softening. "Be careful."

"Hey, it's just baseball," Martin said with a grin. "What's the worst that could happen?"

)))) 🌑 🌑 🌑 ((((

Martin popped a couple of Aleve before he got dressed, and by the time the game started, he felt almost normal. The starting pitcher for the Stars was Kyle Nesbit, a guy who had bounced up and down from the minors to the majors for the better part of his five-year career. While not a battered veteran like Martin, Kyle knew his business, and they'd played together on the Giants. Catching him would be easy. Kyle wouldn't shake off Martin's signs, and Martin was familiar with what Kyle threw: a mediocre fastball and a halfway decent change-up and slider.

When the game started and Martin trotted out onto the field, he glanced over at the bullpen, wondering a) if Andrei was there, and b) who would warm the kid up before he came into the game? The Stars' bullpen catcher was a competent minor-league lifer named Gary Ortega, but Martin doubted Jorge would let him anywhere near Dinescu.

He turned his thoughts to the game. They were playing the Reno Jacks, who were one of the better teams in the Western League. He'd have his hands full.

The first inning went off without a hitch, and Nesbit struck out the first two batters, and then got the Jacks' own bonus baby, a lithe, speedy kid named Wilson Fuchs, to roll over on a slider and ground out.

Martin was the designated hitter batting ninth, and on his first at bat in the third inning, he touched off a deep fly ball the right fielder caught at the warning track. He returned to the dugout, keenly aware he once had the bat speed to hit that ball out.

The game was a tense pitchers' duel, with only zeros and a few weak hits on either side for six innings. Then, in the seventh, who else but Justin Bars strode to the plate. Victor Lowe, the Stars' fleet-footed shortstop, stood on first base after a bunt hit. Everyone stopped what they were doing and watched when Justin came to the plate. He was one of those once-in-a-decade talents you couldn't help being a little awed by.

The Jacks brought in a reliever to face Bars, going by the book with a righty-righty matchup. The reliever was a real fireballer, and his first toss lit up the scoreboard at ninety-seven. Justin watched it sail in, bat on his shoulder, while the ump called, "Strike one." He took another fastball just off the plate for a ball, and then something in his stance changed. It was so minute, few in the stadium saw it. His back foot pivoted out a fraction, and his hands moved up almost imperceptibly on the bat. These tiny adjustments made him a fraction of a second quicker, and when the next heater came in, his bat licked out, and that glorious heavy *THWOCK* filled the stadium. Justin drilled the pitch to right center, a low line drive that cleared the wall by just a couple of feet for a home run.

The crowd went nuts, and Justin accepted the high fives and bear hugs from his teammates with the grace and dignity of baseball royalty when he finished his trot around the bases.

"Had him all the way, huh?" Martin said to Bars and clapped the slugger on the back.

Bars grinned. "I just guessed right on the heater."

"You guessed, huh?" Martin laughed. For guys like Bars, it wasn't just a guess. It bordered on precognition. Sure, they *were* often guessing which pitch would come next, but they were correct more times than they had a right to be.

"Wags!" Jorge shouted over the celebratory din. The Stars' manager summoned Martin with a crooked finger to the other end of the dugout. "Dinescu's pitching the bottom of the seventh."

"Is he warming up?" Martin glanced toward the bull-pen behind the batter's eye.

"Don't get fancy with the signs," Jorge continued, ignoring Martin's question as usual. "Just a number one and location for the fastball, and a number two for the curve-ball."

Before Martin could ask any more questions, the ump's ringing shout of "Strike three!" echoed through the park, and Ian Hawks, the Stars' journeyman third baseman made a U-turn at the plate. The inning was over, the Stars were in the lead, and Andrei Dinescu was about to make his professional debut.

The announcer for Riley Field butchered Andrei's name, making it sound Italian or something. "Now pitching for the Stars, Andrew Dinescah!" The fans were silent as Andrei walked from the bullpen to the mound. Martin wondered if any of them had even been aware he was on the team.

When Andrei reached the mound, Martin went out to meet him, pushing his mask over his head. The Moldovan pitcher no longer looked like the scared, mopey kid Martin had seen a few weeks ago. He was still not a large man, but he had a real presence now. His black hair, which he let hang loose beneath his cap, showed a lustrous sheen. His eyes were bright and alert, and the muscles on his right forearm twitched like steel cables beneath his skin as he clenched the baseball.

Martin stepped onto the mound, and the rest of the Stars' infield—swift shortstop Victor Low, slick-fielding second baseman Luis Perez, stocky first baseman Bryce Cooper, and veteran third baseman Ian Hawks—all moved to join Martin to discuss strategy as was usual when a new pitcher came in. Martin waved them off. He wanted to gauge Andrei's mood before he let anyone else near the pitcher. Martin needn't have worried. Some of the spark left Andrei's eyes, and he stared at the ground, shamefaced. "I am sorry," he said softly. "I did not mean to hurt that man."

"Shreve?" It was a little odd he didn't know the name of his own starting catcher. "Don't worry about it. If anyone had an ass-whooping coming, it was Tanner Fucking Shreve."

"I didn't... I didn't want him to hurt you," Andrei continued. "You have been kind to me."

The admission both touched and embarrassed Martin. "I appreciate the assist," he said lamely, then moved on. "You ready to pitch?"

Andrei nodded and smiled, flashing those too-white teeth. It reminded Martin of something predatory, not so feral as what he'd seen in the locker room, but definitely hungry. "Yes, I feel very strong today."

"Yeah, no shit." Martin chuckled grimly. "Okay, you got the bottom of their order coming up. Soft hitters, except for Shaw. He's a Seattle Mariner on a rehab assignment. He'll sit on your breaking stuff if you let him."

Andrei's eyes went wide, as if Martin had started speaking ancient Greek or something.

"Hey, don't worry about it," Martin said. "It's my job to call the pitches. Just throw what I tell you, and you'll be fine."

Andrei swallowed and nodded.

"Right, now cover your mouth with your glove, like this." Martin held his glove over his face, muffling his voice. It was standard operating procedure for conversations on the mound. Every team feared the other side employed crack lip-readers who could steal signs and strategy from fifty yards away. "We're gonna go over signs, and we don't want anyone to get a sneak peek."

Andrei did as he was told.

"Simple stuff. If I put down a one, that's a fastball. I'll make another motion to tell you where I want it. If I put a two down, that's your curveball. Make sense?"

Andrei let out a long, relieved breath. "I understand."

The home-plate umpire had started his slow, deliberate journey toward the mound to break up Martin's meeting and get the game rolling. Martin turned and gave him a thumbs-up, then trotted back to the plate.

He squatted behind the dish and held up three fingers, indicating Andrei should make three warm-up tosses. The Moldovan brought his glove and the ball to his waist, kicked, and fired.

After ten years as a catcher, Martin knew pitches made different sounds depending on the velocity. A ninety-mile-per-hour fastball hummed. A ninety-five-mile-per-hour fastball buzzed, and a pitch approaching triple digits *hissed.* The first warm-up pitch Andrei Dinescu threw to Martin came in like an angry snake and popped the glove like a shotgun blast. He flinched as he caught it, trembling from adrenaline, surprise, and plain, old fear. He looked up at the scoreboard. The pitch speed read 97.

Martin took the ball from his mitt and stared at it like it was some species of meteor fallen from the heavens and not hurled from the strange little pitcher sixty feet, six inches away. The Stars' infielders also goggled. They'd heard that pitch come in, too.

"Hey, you wanna finish up those warm-up tosses," the umpire said. He was an older guy, pushing fifty, with a dour face and a bit of a gut. He had that slightly out-of-shape, slightly pissed-off look that a lot of umps had.

"Uh, yeah, sorry," Martin said and tossed the ball back. Andrei deftly swiped it out of the air.

The next pitch practically screamed to home plate. This time the scoreboard read 98. The third pitch came in at 99. Martin supposed he should have expected this after what had happened in the locker room. What really ate at him, though, was now he understood why Jorge and the Giants organization were so hush-hush with the kid, why he hadn't been allowed to throw in a live game yet, and why they were keeping him all but hidden from his teammates. It didn't feel miraculous; it felt *wrong.*

The umpire took up his position behind Martin, and the first Mountaineer batter stepped up to the plate, a weak-hitting Mariners prospect named Joseph Highfield. He was one of those guys you want to tell to hang it up. To grab them and shout the awful truth that they'll never make the big leagues. You don't because there's that constant lurking horror that it could be someone grabbing and shouting at you one day.

The ump pointed at Andrei and said, "Play ball."

Highfield took up his stance in the right-hand box. Martin put one finger down and patted his left thigh—fastball, outside corner.

Andrei nodded and fired a fastball. It buzzed in and hit the mitt exactly where Martin had set up. That kind of control and the kind of velocity were rarely on speaking terms.

The ump pointed a finger and said, "Strike one."

Highfield stared at the spot where the ball had come in like it just materialized there. "Looked a little outside," he said weakly.

"Yeah, like you fuckin' saw it," Martin said as he threw the ball back. The ump chuckled.

Highfield made a pouting face but kept his mouth shut. He made a feeble swipe at the next pitch, a 99-mile-per-hour missile that was by him before he started his swing. He just watched the third pitch come straight down the middle, the very picture of defeat when he turned away from the plate before the ump even called strike three.

"Kid can throw," the umpire said.

"He sure can," Martin agreed. *It's what else he might do that scares me.*

The next batter strode to the plate with a swagger and confidence wholly out of place in the minor leagues. Tall and rail thin, Felix Shaw had dark brown skin, long spidery arms, and a mouth turned down in what seemed a perpetual frown. He was a solid major-league outfielder who'd spent the last four years with the Mariners. He'd torn the meniscus in his right knee at the end of last season and was working his way through a rehab stint before rejoining the big club.

"Hey, Wags," Shaw said as he stepped to the plate, offering Martin a genuine smile. Despite Shaw's serious demeanor, he was a nice guy. He and Martin had played together for half a season before Martin signed with the Giants.

"What's up, Shaw? How's the knee?" Martin said, looking up from his crouch.

Shaw chuckled as he took up his stance. "I'd complain, but I don't have to squat on the fucking thing."

Martin laughed and realized he hadn't felt his knees at all since he'd entered the game. He supposed a truckload of adrenaline will do that to you. Shaw's comment seemed to remind his battered joints to pipe up, and they did, with a low, grinding ache. Martin put down one finger again and tapped his left thigh. "Get ready, man," Martin said to Shaw.

Shaw grunted, and his face resumed that dour frown, which was just concentration and focus. Andrei delivered the pitch with the same rising hiss as the last three. It popped the mitt on the inside part of the plate, causing Shaw to flinch back.

"Ball, inside," the ump said.

Martin grimaced. That pitch had caught the corner, but Shaw was a big leaguer, and a minor league ump was going to give him all kinds of leeway.

"Shit," Shaw said, staring out at the mound. "Where the fuck this kid come from?"

Martin threw the ball back and shook his head. 'You wouldn't believe me."

"Bonus baby?" Shaw said, staring appraisingly at the mound.

"Something like that." Martin resumed his crouch. He put down the next sign. This time he called for a fastball in the upper part of the zone, hoping to induce a swing and miss from Shaw. Thing is, a 99-mile-per-hour fastball is impressive, but it's not unusual in the major leagues. It's not even all that uncommon. Good hitters can time a pitch like that. Shaw was a good hitter.

Again, Andrei delivered the pitch exactly where Martin called for it, but Shaw somehow managed to get on top of the ball rather than hitting it straight up in the air, which usually happens when a batter makes contact with a shoulder-high pitch. Instead, he hit an absolute rocket right back at the pitcher's mound, a baseball-shaped missile traveling at an easy 110 miles per hour. Most pitchers would get out of the way and let a fielder handle that kind of smash after it had slowed. Andrei just stuck his glove out so fast Martin didn't see it move. He heard the ball hit the leather, though, with a sharp *THWAP*.

Shaw had taken a few steps out of the batter's box before he realized what had happened. He turned to Martin. "Did he fucking catch that?"

Martin nodded dumbly, and the umpire had enough composure to raise his right fist and call Shaw out.

Inexplicably, Andrei tossed the ball to first base. Bryce Cooper caught it dutifully but shot a confused glance at his pitcher. Bryce tossed the ball back to Andrei, and that bewildered look reappeared on his face. Martin called time and jogged to the mound.

"Nice catch, kid," Martin said. "You know you don't need to throw to first when you catch it in the air."

"Oh, yes," Andrei said and blushed. "I forgot."

How Andrei could forget a fundamental aspect of the game was beyond Martin, but he said, "No worries. Let's get the next guy and keep your ERA at zero."

Again, that absolutely befuddled expression. Martin felt pretty sure Andrei had no idea what an ERA was. Martin turned to head back to the plate when Jorge exited the dugout and shouted for time.

The Stars' manager took a slow, leisurely pace to the mound, and Andrei's body language changed. The confidence, the fire, all of that drained out of him. His shoulders rounded and hunched, his head hung, and he refused to look at his manager.

"Nice work, Andrei," Jorge said and held his hand out for the ball.

"You're not gonna let him finish the inning?" Martin asked.

Jorge shook his head. "I saw everything I needed to."

Andrei meekly held out the ball, and Jorge took it.

What Steph had said about Andrei being some kind of lab rat came back to Martin. He imagined the animals put through tortuous experiments by pharmaceutical companies and the like probably behaved a lot like Andrei. Sudden protective rage seized Martin. The kid was almost certainly getting the shit end of whatever the Giants organization was doing with him. *To* him.

Jorge motioned with his left hand to the bullpen, calling for a lefty reliever.

Martin glared at his manager. "Kid throws ninety-eight now, huh, Skip?"

"You saw the pitch speed, didn't you?" Jorge said.

The bullpen gate opened, and Oliver Yang jogged through and toward the mound. Now Andrei finally looked up at his manager, eyes hooded, demure, whipped.

"Hit the showers," Jorge said, and Andrei trudged off toward the dugout.

Martin wanted to say more, maybe to ask his manager why he didn't seem surprised that his new pitcher had developed one of the best fastballs in the league in two weeks. But Oliver Yang trotted up to the mound. Jorge handed him the ball, then unceremoniously departed.

"Holy crap, that new guy can bring it, huh?" Yang said with a big grin. The Stars' reliever always used words like "crap" or "frigging" like some daring fifth grader afraid he might get in trouble for cursing.

"Yeah," Martin said distantly, watching Andrei disappear down the dugout steps and then down the tunnel. Jorge took up a position at the head of the tunnel, a lone knight at the mouth of the dragon's cave. But who was he protecting? The peasants or the dragon?

May 26th

On the last day of the homestand, Martin was again summoned to Jorge's office. This time, the Stars' manager stood behind his desk and seemed nervous, even agitated.

"I'm starting him tonight," Jorge said before Martin could sit down.

"Dinescu?" Martin asked, alarmed. If Dinescu was starting, Martin was catching, and that sent a ragged chill down his back. Each time the kid threw the ball, things got stranger. He threw harder, of course, but his entire demeanor changed, too. The fact he was, once again, completely MIA since his short stint in relief a week ago did little to assuage Martin's growing dread. He'd asked Steph a few days ago if Andrei had been into the gym. He hadn't. In fact, no one had seen him.

"Yes, Dinescu," Jorge snapped, his voice rough and sharp at the same time. For a man who never displayed an iota of emotion, he all but seethed with it now.

Martin drew in a deep breath and let it out. "You know, Skip, maybe it's time you tell me what the fuck is going on."

Martin expected another rebuke. Hell, as hard as he'd been pushing at the Stars' little secret, he wouldn't be surprised if Jorge cut him right here. Over the past week, he'd come to the conclusion that he didn't care. The Giants and Jorge were hiding something dangerous. Jorge mumbled something in Spanish under his breath. His face softened, and he leaned against his desk like he needed it for support. "After tonight, I will. I promise."

The admission and the sudden and absolute exhaustion in his manager's voice shocked Martin. "Why after tonight?"

"I…I can't tell you," he said. "This comes from the top, but if tonight goes well, it could be good for everyone, you included."

Martin blinked. There was a conspiratorial atmosphere in the office. "The kid's dangerous, right?" Martin said. "Don't try and deny it. Just tell me how dangerous."

Jorge rubbed at his face and then collapsed into his chair. "Yes, he could be, but with you behind the plate… and a few other things, it will be fine."

"And if it isn't?" Martin asked.

Jorge looked away, and Martin noticed the circles under the man's eyes. However difficult the mystery of Andrei Dinescu had been for Martin, his manager was getting a double dose.

"Look, Jorge," Martin began. "Give me a reason why I shouldn't walk out of this office right now and retire?" *Other than the fact I'm drowning in debt and literally have no other skills outside of baseball.*

Jorge met Martin's gaze, his eyes chips of dark stone. "I'll give you one. Andrei likes you; he *protected* you. That means he'll listen to you more than anyone else if things get out of hand." Jorge stared at him fixedly. "People are safer with you behind the dish. You get me?"

Jorge was playing on Martin's sense of duty, his sense of community, and counting on him to make the necessary choice out of devotion to his team. Martin wanted to punch him in the face for being right.

Jorge reached under his desk and took out a cardboard box, Planters Sunflower Seeds printed on the side of it. Instead of every ballplayer's favorite on-field snack, it held a rosin bag—a white cloth sack filled with a drying agent pitchers used to keep a grip on the baseball—as well as a small medallion on a silver chain and a dog-eared copy of the *Old Farmer's Almanac*, probably the same one Jorge had been reading when he initially told Martin about Andrei Dinescu.

Jorge set the box on the desk, picked up the rosin bag, and tossed it to Martin. It released a puff of white dust and a strong herbal smell, slightly medicinal. "What's in this?" Martin asked. Rosin generally didn't smell like anything.

"Something special," Jorge said. "Tonight, when Andrei gets, uh, wild, tell him to go to his rosin bag. He'll have one just like this."

The way Jorge used the word "wild" caused Martin's testicles to draw up into his belly. He was sure Jorge meant wild, as in miss-the-strike-zone wild; he was also sure Jorge meant something a lot worse. "And if he doesn't?"

Jorge handed Martin the medallion. It was heavy and looked like polished steel, or perhaps silver. On its face was a stylized medieval bust of a bearded man, maybe a priest, and on the reverse was a series of words around the circumference. Martin couldn't pronounce them, but he recognized them. They were the words Jorge had shouted to keep Andrei from twisting off Tanner Shreve's head.

"What is all this?" Martin asked.

"Protection. The words on the back are pronounced like this: *Sângele lui Ailbe*. Say them back."

Martin did and butchered them.

"Again," Jorge prodded.

Martin did better the second time, but Jorge drilled him until he had them right. "What is this? Is it like some kind of..." Martin laughed and shook his head. He'd almost said spell. "This is starting to feel pretty goddamn stupid."

"Not stupid. Necessary. You've seen what the kid can do," Jorge said. "But you really haven't seen anything yet. You need all this. Now put the talisman around your neck."

Martin *really* didn't like the word talisman, but he tucked the medallion under his shirt.

"If you need to, say the words and then tell Andrei to stop what he's doing," Jorge said.

"What will he be doing?" Martin said. "And how will I know?"

"You'll know," Jorge replied cryptically.

Martin pointed at the copy of the *Old Farmer's Almanac*. "And that?"

"That's mine," Jorge replied, putting the box and book back under his desk.

"Why do I feel like you're sending me off to war?" Martin said.

"Baseball is always a war," Jorge said.

)➤➤●●((

Martin had a hundred questions, but all his manager would say was, "Wait until after the game." He gave up and went from the manager's office to the gym, hoping to find

Steph there. The weight of all the crazy shit he'd just been told felt like a hundred pounds sitting square on his chest. Steph wasn't in the gym, and Martin was somewhat grateful. She'd certainly tell him not to play tonight, not to indulge whatever Jorge and the Giants' brass were up to. He had to admit he was curious, maybe destructively so.

He went to the clubhouse and sat down in front of his locker. The game started at 7:00 p.m., and he'd come in early enough that most of the other players hadn't shown up yet. Only Bryce Cooper, the first baseman, and Victor Lowe, the shortstop, were in the locker room. They cast wary glances at him. That was the other part of this horse-shit that aggravated him. All the mystery around Andrei Dinescu and Martin's part in it had made him a pariah. It wasn't terribly overt. No one said anything, but he hadn't been invited for after-game drinks or dinner since Andrei's relief appearance.

Despite whatever happened tonight, he was likely through with the Sacramento Stars. He opened his locker to get his headphones. They were where he'd left them in his locker, but they sat atop a sizable manilla envelope that hadn't been there before. He drew in a sharp breath at its sudden and unwelcome appearance.

He moved closer to his locker, blocking anyone from seeing into it. The envelope was blank, but when he picked it up, its weight only increased Martin's dread. He opened it, hands shaking, and reached inside, fully expecting the mysterious envelope to be filled with poisonous spiders or something. His fingers brushed cool metal, and he grasped the object and pulled it out. It was a knife—a dagger, really—about six inches long with an ornate brass hilt. The blade shone lustrous and pure even in the shadows of his locker. A scrap of paper was affixed to the hilt with a rubber band. Martin pulled it off and unfurled it. Someone had written three words in simple block letters: NO WILD PITCHES.

Martin shoved the knife and note back into the envelope. Who had put it there? Who knew? Of the coaches, only Julian Tate seemed to really know what was going on, and Tater had seemed outright afraid of Andrei. Mike Embrey had never even mentioned Dinescu, which meant he either didn't know much about him, which seemed unlikely, or had been offered some compensation for silence and cooperation. He supposed one of the other players could have placed the knife, but their exposure to Andrei had been minimal and carefully controlled.

The real question was, of course, did he need the knife?

Fuck, fuck, fuck. Martin rapped his forehead against the locker in frustration. Whatever Andrei was—the knife and its lustrous metal gave him a pretty good idea—the thought of shivving the kid on the mound was not something he could exactly wrap his head around. Then he factored in Jorge's frayed demeanor and the fucking *talisman* he wore around his neck, and the knife didn't seem such a terrible idea. In fact, it and NO WILD PITCHES seemed to be the best advice he'd received all day.

Instead of reaching for the knife or his headphones or even his uniform, Martin reached for his bottle of little white pills, shook three into his hand, and dry-swallowed the Percocet. Yeah, his knees hurt, and yeah, the narcotics would help him on the field, but he'd been taking more and more primarily because they fought away the specters of doubt and the haunting apparitions of his many failings. They numbed everything, made things more manageable, and that was the only way he could see strapping on the gear and catching Andrei Dinescu for his first start.

The Stars were playing the number one team in the division that night, the Salt Lake Halos. They were a Los Angeles Angels farm team and featured such a wealth of talented prospects they could almost field a serviceable big-league team on their own. They had owned the Stars in the season series by a count of six wins to one loss and were starting their absolute best pitcher tonight, a kid named Jonathan O'Leary, a six-foot-six, baby-faced twenty-year-old from Omaha, Nebraska, with a fastball that occasionally touched triple digits.

As Martin stepped onto the field in the fading sun-shine of an early June evening, feeling much better thanks to a wave of narcotic-induced euphoria, he idly wondered if Jorge had saved Andrei's start for the best team. Then he looked up at the sky, saw the faint outline of the full moon, and knew the team Andrei faced had exactly zero to do with anything.

For once, Andrei sat on the dugout bench flanked by Jorge and Tater. Jorge seemed to have regained his composure, but Tater looked like he might crawl out of his skin. The pitching coach cast fearful, sidelong glances at his starting pitcher and looked to be fighting every single instinct he possessed not to jump up and run. Andrei sat up straight, his hair cascading around his shoulders in gleaming tides of liquid black. It reminded Martin of a mane. Andrei's mouth was set in a hard line, and his eyes were black bullet holes framed by white sclera. He held a rosin bag in his pitching hand.

The game would start soon, and the rest of the Stars had taken the field. Martin stood behind home plate, waiting for Andrei to take the mound and warm up. He looked at Jorge and held his hands out, palms up. *We doing this*?

The Stars' manager said something to Andrei, who then rose slowly from the bench. He climbed the dugout stairs, seemed to see the five or so thousand people in the stands for the first time, flinched, and bared his teeth.

He's not even gonna make it to the mound, Martin thought, and the paltry weight of the dagger duct-taped to the underside of his chest protector suddenly felt like a couple hundred pounds. He'd positioned it so he could easily reach beneath the protector and rip the knife free.

Andrei lifted his rosin bag to his nose, closed his eyes, and inhaled deeply. He seemed to get himself under control after that and trotted to the mound, his steps bounding and fluid.

Martin squatted behind the plate and held up five fingers. Five warm-up pitches. He assumed Andrei had done a complete warm-up with someone before the game, but he had no way of knowing.

Andrei dropped the rosin bag on the mound behind

him, came set in a single graceful motion, balanced and perfect, and flung a fastball that didn't hum or hiss. He fired a baseball that *howled* between the mound and home plate.

The white meteor slapped Martin's mitt hard enough to leave his palm numb and tingling. Instinctively, he jerked his head up to see the pitch speed on the scoreboard. That section of the Stars' board was blank—because of course it was. The Giants' new rookie sensation had likely thrown one of the fastest pitches ever recorded, and that kind of thing attracted a lot of attention. Unwanted attention.

That tide of calm euphoria Martin had been riding waned, then ended completely when the next four pitches came in as hard and fast and accurate as the first. Of course, pitches thrown that hard were more than a little noticeable, radar gun or not. The crowd had quieted, and Martin could feel the startled gazes from players in both dugouts. Some of them were going to have to step into the box and try to hit against Andrei. *Lots of luck, fellas.*

The word "wild" popped into Martin's head as the ump took up his position behind him, and the first Halos batter strode to the plate, a good-looking, muscular kid named Manny Soler. If Andrei missed and hit someone with one of his record-setting fastballs, it could be bad, very bad. Only one player in the history of baseball had ever been killed by a thrown pitch, and that had happened before helmets became mandatory. Martin felt the chances of a second fatality were as high as they'd ever been in the history of the sport, and not just because Andrei's pitches were practically leaving vapor trails.

Soler nodded a greeting to Martin and the umpire, then took up his stance in the left-hand batter's box. *Here we go,* Martin thought and put down the number one. He didn't indicate a location. He didn't think it mattered.

Andrei looked in, eyes gleaming in the fading sun, came set, kicked, and fired. Another white comet flashed from mound to plate, and Martin knew he'd have to put on a couple of batting gloves under his catcher's mitt between innings or suffer a bone bruise.

The ump didn't call the pitch for a few seconds, and Soler just stared out at the mound like Andrei had fired a gun at him. Finally, the umpire pointed and said, "Strike one." The slight questioning note to the call told Martin the ump hadn't seen the pitch come in.

The stadium quieted, and all eyes in both dugouts and the stands were fixed on the man on the mound. He wasn't wearing that attention well. Andrei paced and stamped and cast fretful looks at the sky.

Martin threw the ball back to get his pitcher's attention. Andrei caught it, and Martin made the *whoa*-ing motion with both hands, universal catcher sign language for calm down and get your shit together.

Andrei went to his rosin bag, bringing it to his nose like he'd done before. That seemed to do the trick, and he visibly calmed. He then struck out Soler with two more blistering fastballs.

The rest of the first inning went by in six more pitches, all strikes. There's a term for when a pitcher strikes out all three batters on just nine pitches. It's called an immaculate inning, and it's a celebrated occurrence. No one seemed in the mood for celebration when Martin and Andrei went into the dugout between innings. In fact, the place was tomb-silent. Andrei sat next to Jorge, looking at the ground, and Martin sat next to him.

No one offered words of encouragement or congratulations. No one came near them. That actually made Martin feel better. Folks might not know exactly what Andrei was or the kind of danger he represented, but baseball players, being as superstitious as they were, avoided anything that even looked like bad magic.

"Good work," Jorge said softly to Andrei, though he looked right at Martin.

In the bottom of the first, the Stars fared poorly against Jonathan O'Leary, the Halos' starter, though his dominance appeared to be only the regular human kind. He needed thirteen pitches to retire the first three Stars batters, striking out two and getting the mighty Justin Bars to fly out softly to right.

Then it was back on the field and back behind the dish. The first two Halos to bat struck out, though Andrei threw his first ball of the game, another screaming fastball just above the top of the strike zone.

The last batter in the top of the second was the Halos' first baseman, Terrance Calhoun, one of those guys often referred to as a "quadruple-A" player. Of course, the minor leagues only go to Triple-A, and then it's the majors. The quadruple-A player is a guy who dominates the farm system but can't make the cut in the majors. They tend to go up and down for a time before they give up, find employment in Korea or Japan in their professional leagues, or, like Calhoun, hang around, grimly, with a giant chip on their shoulder and a real hatred for kids with the talent to make it all the way to the bigs.

Calhoun was a short, thick guy with a barrel chest and a gut that had grown steadily over the last few seasons. He had the face of a bully, equal parts midwestern pale and California sunburned, a squashed nose, small shark-like eyes, and a mouth that seemed to be perpetually smiling. There was never any joy in that smile, though; it was just cover for the asshole lurking beneath it. That asshole stepped up and said hello as soon as Calhoun stepped into the box. "Got a real hot-shit bonus baby out there, huh, Wags?"

Martin knew Calhoun mostly by reputation, but he'd been with the Giants the last time Calhoun had been called up to the Angels, failed miserably, and got shipped back down again. "He's got skills, yeah," Martin said.

"I'm about to take those fucking skills over the left-field fence," Calhoun said and spat a stream of tobacco juice too close to Martin's right foot.

"Uh-huh," Martin said. "Tell you what, man. You make contact with one fucking pitch, even a foul ball, and I'll give you five hundred bucks."

"Gentlemen, enough," the umpire said.

"You're on, Wags," Calhoun said and took up his stance, an ugly, simple thing that relied almost completely on hand and wrist speed, of which Calhoun was in short and declining supply.

Martin looked out at the mound. Andrei was pacing more between pitches, looking jittery, and he hadn't touched his rosin bag in a while. It wasn't the time to fuck around, but Calhoun had gotten to Martin, chewed through weakened defenses that would normally have rebuffed the attempts of a bloated piece of shit like Calhoun to rattle him. He did something stupid. He put down the ol' number one and patted his right thigh. Fastball inside.

Andrei delivered the pitch, another one that felt more like a gunshot than anything thrown by a human being. It came nowhere near hitting Calhoun, but the giant fucking tool jumped back with a growl. The ump called the pitch a ball, and Calhoun glared out at the mound. "You keep that shit over the plate!" Calhoun yelled and pointed at Andrei. His teammates in the Halos dugout echoed Calhoun's outrage, shouting and cursing, likely hoping the Stars' currently unhittable pitcher would get tossed.

Andrei stared back, his lips pulled away from his teeth, mouth crooked in a slight smile.

Oh, fuck me, Martin thought and shot up from his crouch. He put an arm around Calhoun's waist. "Hey, man, no intent there. Pitch just got away from him."

Calhoun threw one more withering glare at the mound and took up his stance again. "You better tell that kid not to fuck around," he said to Martin. "I don't play that shit."

"I gotcha, Calhoun," Martin said. The memory of Andrei pinning another gigantic asshole to a locker with one hand and nearly strangling him to death rose up like a corpse floating to the surface of a still pond. That had been a week ago, and Andrei had manhandled Shreve with childlike ease. *What could he do now?* Martin shuddered, slid his hand beneath his chest protector, and touched the knife taped there.

As it turned out, Martin did not end up owing Calhoun five hundred bucks. He struck out on the next three
pitches without making contact. Before the Halos' resident
fuck-stick could say anything, Martin popped up and met
Andrei walking in from the mound.

"You okay, kid?" Martin asked.

"That man wanted to fight me," Andrei whispered,
his face still set in that rictus snarl. "I smelled it."

Martin heard no fear in the Moldovan's voice. Instead, he noted a perverse longing that made him very aware
just how full his bladder was. "Hey, we're not fighting; we're
pitching."

Andrei's gaze was fixed on the Halos' dugout. That
would not do.

"Hey!" Martin barked as they made the dugout steps,
and Andrei's head snapped around, snake-fast. "You hear
me?"

Andrei nodded and took his seat next to Jorge. "What
the fuck happened out there?" the Stars' manager said.

"Oh, you know, Calhoun being a dick," Martin said.
"I got it under control."

Jorge cast another worried glance at Andrei. "Keep
it that way. Both of you."

Andrei said nothing, but his hands clenched and unclenched, clenched and unclenched. He sure as shit didn't
look like someone *under control*.

O'Leary retired the next three Stars batters in order,
and when Martin took the field in the top of the third, the
sky had darkened, and they had a new spectator: the bright

spotlight of a very full moon.

Andrei Dinescu was throwing a no-hitter through four innings. No, check that; he was throwing a perfect game. Only one Halos batter managed to even put wood on the ball, and that had been a soft grounder to Victor Lowe at shortstop, who threw the runner out with ease.

Martin had come up to bat in the bottom of third, with a runner on second, and then, miracle of miracles, O'Leary hung a curveball, and Martin didn't miss it. He experienced that beautiful, effortless contact that feels like nothing at all until you see the ball rocket off into the sky. He missed a homerun by inches as the ball smashed into the top of the right-field fence and bounced back. It turned into a double and scored the runner from second, giving the Stars a one-run lead. They still clung to that lead as they took the field in the top of the fifth.

Night had descended, and the moon shone down on the field like a spotlight, highlighting the drama playing out on the mound, spurring it on. Andrei had maintained his composure for the most part, though he all but quivered with energy between pitches, pacing, jumping at the slightest sound from the stands.

Andrei disposed of the first two batters with ease, a strike out and a weak pop-up to first baseman Bryce Cooper. The third batter for the Halos in the fifth was their old pal Terrance Calhoun. The strike out on his first at-bat clearly hadn't sat well with him. In his second turn at the plate, the veteran's usual shit-eating smile was nowhere to be found, and his jaw muscles bunched like he was trying to chew something particularly tough to swallow. Martin could all but feel the sizzling rage on the man, and the hairs on the nape of his neck stood up straight and stiff.

Calhoun said nothing as he stepped into the box, but Andrei reacted to the presence of the big first baseman immediately. That wild agitation ceased, and he became still and focused, his eyes locked on the man in the box like a lion might stare down its prey. Martin shook his head and groaned, then said, "Time."

"Go ahead," the ump said. Calhoun tossed Martin a glare as he trotted out to the mound. Andrei's eyes never wavered from Halo's first baseman as Martin approached.

"Andrei," Martin said and wrinkled his nose. The kid had worked up a lather, and his uniform shirt clung to his back and chest. The smell coming off him reeked thick and musk-like. Definitely not your typical sweat smell. "Andrei, fucking look at me."

The pitcher finally pulled his gaze from Calhoun, who, like the colossal dipshit he was, stared back with stubborn defiance. "This man is still angry," Andrei said, his voice low and rumbling. He breathed in deeply through his nose, and his eyes rolled back into his head. "Ohhhhh, and afraid."

Martin suppressed the shudder climbing up his back. "Look, one more out and you qualify for the win," Martin said softly. "Let's get Calhoun, and then you can hit the showers." Martin had every intention of recommending

Jorge pull the kid after this inning. They were definitely playing with fire, and he hoped the Stars' manager had seen enough. Martin sure had.

"I am…having trouble," Andrei said and stared up at the moon.

Those words increased Martin's shudders to full-blown shakes, and all the spit dried up in his mouth. "Go to your rosin bag, Andrei."

Andrei turned and stared at the bag. "It makes me sick. Like medicine."

"I don't give a fuck," Martin said, fear making him reckless. That and the fact the umpire had started moving toward the mound to break up their meeting. He didn't want another person anywhere near Andrei right now. "Go to your bag, Andrei." He remembered the medallion beneath his uniform, the one with the bust of the bearded priest and the strange words in Romanian. He wondered if he could get to it before the umpire reached them. Luckily, he didn't have to. Andrei turned away, stalked to the back of the mound, and picked up his rosin bag. He brought it to his nose and breathed deep.

"Why is he doing that?" the umpire asked, a quizzical frown on his face.

Martin put his arm around the ump's shoulders and ushered him back toward home plate. "Who the fuck knows? I'm just supposed to make sure he throws strikes."

"He sure does that," the umpire said as they reached home plate.

"You girls have a nice chat?" Calhoun said, standing in the batter's box, one thumb hooked in his belt, bat cocked over his shoulder. If there were any other pitcher on the mound, Martin would call for the next fastball in Calhoun's ear. With Andrei out there, and the full moon glaring down on them, that'd pretty much be attempted murder.

"Fuck you, Calhoun," Martin said and pulled his mask down over his face. "Maybe you'd stick in the majors more than five minutes if you weren't such a giant prick."

Calhoun's eyes went wide, and his mouth trembled. Martin had aimed well and scored a direct hit.

"One more word out of you, Calhoun, and I'll toss you. I swear to God," the ump said, and Calhoun somehow held his tongue. Martin looked back at the ump, grateful, and the man nodded. "Let's play ball." He pointed at Andrei, indicating he could deliver the next pitch.

Martin called for another fastball—he hadn't bothered with much else all night since not a single Halo had managed to do more than strike out or make weak contact. Andrei came set, wound up, and tossed a whistling baseball a foot over Calhoun's head. Martin had no doubt Andrei could have caved in Calhoun's skull with that pitch. The kid had pinpoint control. He'd actually shown remarkable restraint by *not* beaning Calhoun. The Halos' husky first baseman didn't see it that way.

"Cocksucker," Calhoun hissed, that shitty smile blooming on his face. He now had righteous cause to do something colossally stupid. Martin jumped up from his crouch and tried to grab Calhoun as the Halos' first baseman flung his bat aside and charged the mound. Martin caught Calhoun's jersey with one reaching hand, but the man twisted free and ran headlong at Andrei.

Normally, in such a situation, the dugouts and bull-pens would empty, and a flood of players from both teams would pour onto the field. This scrum was generally harmless, and for the most part, it separated the two aggrieved players from each other with a tide of bodies. In this case, no one moved for the space of a few heartbeats, and the crowd drew in a collective gasp. Calhoun gained the mound where Andrei stood waiting, white teeth bared and gleaming in the acrid glare of the stadium lights.

Calhoun might have sensed something was wrong when he got within striking distance of his target because he faltered for just a moment. Later, Martin would think it was the smell coming off Andrei that did it. That terrible musky odor. The Halos' first baseman threw a clumsy haymaker at Andrei, who didn't avoid the blow. Calhoun's fist connected, whipping Andrei's head to the side. Calhoun didn't get a chance for a second strike.

Andrei's right hand snaked up, grabbed Calhoun's right forearm, and twisted. Martin, who was charging after Calhoun, heard the bone snap from ten feet away, and everyone in the stadium heard the man's high, wailing scream.

As much as he despised Calhoun, Martin didn't want to watch him get torn apart by...well, the word lurked in his head, but he couldn't bring himself to even think it. Martin barreled past Calhoun—he'd never pry the man loose from Andrei's herculean grip—and hit his pitcher in a full-body tackle. It was like running into a wall, a wall of solid muscle and feral strength. The impact rattled Martin's teeth, and stars bloomed before his eyes, but his weight and momentum were enough to tear Andrei free of Calhoun and carry them both to the ground.

Martin landed on top of his pitcher and wrapped his arms around him. "Andrei, calm down!" he shouted over Calhoun's desperate screaming and the mingled shouts of forty-some ballplayers storming in their direction.

Andrei thrashed violently, and suddenly Martin found himself on his back with his pitcher atop him. Andrei pinned Martin to the ground with one hand, his eyes blackened pits of hunger and fury. Above his head, the full moon gloated. Andrei pulled back one hand; the nails on that hand had grown long, thick, and sharp, like the talons of a beast.

Martin saw the other players clustered around Calhoun, and the usual pushing and shoving had commenced. For the most part, he and Andrei were alone, though he could see Jorge trying to make his way to them. The Stars' manager shouted something, but it was lost in the din of players arguing and spectators cheering on the fracas.

Andrei hadn't struck yet, and he stared down at Martin, his face pinched with rage and something else... Frustration? He was fighting it. His muscles quaked with the effort of rebelling against his nature and the terrible pull of the moon. Martin reached under his chest protector and gripped the hilt of the knife. Then Andrei spoke.

"Wags. Help...me...please," the pitcher whispered. His voice rippled with pain and fury and awful, bottomless grief.

Martin's fist closed tighter on the hilt of the knife, and he knew he had a window to pull it out and drive it into Andrei's chest. "Fuck, kid," he said, some of Andrei's sadness mingling with his own decades-long depression.

How many times had he wished someone would save him from his own terrible decisions, show him a moment of kindness, toss him a rope on the stormy sea of his failed marriage and declining career? A tear slid down his cheek, and he let go of the knife and reached beneath his uniform shirt. He pulled the talisman free and held it in front of Andrei's face. The pitcher recoiled and brought his hand back to strike again.

"*Sângele lui Ailbe!*" Martin shouted, and like that day in the locker room, Andrei shut down immediately, arms dropping to his sides, eyes glazed and vacant. "Go to your rosin bag."

Andrei rolled off Martin and crawled to the back of the mound. The scrum had reached them at this point, and bodies piled on Martin, but he saw Andrei push the rosin bag up to his nose and breath deep before he, too, disappeared beneath a tide of angry, cursing ballplayers.

Martin waited for the field to erupt into a scene of terrible violence as Andrei ripped into his attackers, but it didn't happen. The pitcher lay at the bottom of the pile, sucking in the herbal stink of his rosin bag.

Both managers and the umpire were shouting for everyone to calm down, and the field quieted. Jorge grabbed Martin's hand and pulled him up. The Stars' manager's face was pale with sick fear. "You okay, Wags?"

Martin ignored him and rushed to pull people off Andrei. After seeing Calhoun's injury, most of them didn't have much will to actually tangle with the pitcher. Andrei lay on the mound, curled into a fetal position, softly weeping beneath the staring eye of the moon.

Jorge joined Martin as he helped Andrei to his feet. The kid was shaking, his face streaked with snot and tears, and he clutched his rosin bag in a death grip.

Martin put an arm around Andrei's shoulders and glared at Jorge. "I think it's time for a pitching change, Skip."

A trainer Martin had never seen before popped out of the dugout and raced toward the mound. He was a big, burly guy with a shaved head and a crooked nose. He looked more like a hitman from a movie about the Russian mob than a medical professional.

"I will take him," the trainer said, his Russian accent so thick Martin thought for a second it was an act.

"Go with him, Andrei," Jorge said, and the mountainous trainer gently led Andrei off the field, one hand on his back, like a man might handle a spooked animal. The scrum had ended, and many of the players on both sides were now just standing on the field, looking shell-shocked, mostly because they'd caught sight of Calhoun's grotesque injury. The Halos' first baseman lay on a golf cart stretcher, face white as paper, holding his right arm, which bent at a ghoulish angle halfway down his forearm. The Halos' training staff were trying to keep the limb immobilized.

As Calhoun was driven off the field, Jorge signaled to the bullpen for a right-handed reliever. "Can you catch the rest of the game?" he asked.

Martin laughed. "Do I have a choice?"

The Stars won the game one to nothing, mainly because the Halos had simply lost the will to play. No one wanted to be on the field any longer than they had to.

When the game ended, there was no celebration, just a bunch of horrified ballplayers trudging back to the clubhouse. No one said a word, and everyone steadfastly avoided Martin, though a few frightened and angry glances were thrown his way.

As Martin collapsed on the stool in front of his locker, the sheathed knife under his chest protector dug into his stomach. Should he have used it? Now, removed from the terror of what had happened on the mound, stabbing his pitcher to death in front of God and everyone seemed an absurd idea.

He was about to take his gear off when he saw Jorge moving through the locker room toward him. He rolled his eyes as his manager approached. "What the fuck do you want?" He was done treating Jorge with anything bordering on respect. Martin knew he was finished with the Stars and with baseball, so what was the point?

"I know you're angry," Jorge began, hands spread wide in a conciliatory gesture.

Martin hadn't expected this opening, but it just pissed him off. "Angry?" he hissed. "I'm a little past angry, Skip. I almost got killed by a goddamn—"

"Don't," Jorge warned. Martin held his tongue because that single word was so laced with terror that it snuffed out Martin's rage like a bucket of water over a campfire.

Most of the players in the locker room were staring at them, faces a mixture of fear and doubt—and, yes, anger, too. They knew something terrible had happened. *Was* happening.

"Come with me," Jorge said.

"Why in the world would I do that?" Martin said, trying to sound defiant, but it just came out as bone-weary. His knees hurt like a bastard, and he just wanted to take a handful of Percocet and disappear into narcotic oblivion.

"You have a meeting in the front office," Jorge said.

That meant upstairs, where the people who didn't wear uniforms but ran the team did their business. The scouts, the general manager, the people who worked for the big club in San Francisco. "Who with?" Martin said.

"Do you want answers or not?" Jorge offered.

"Fuck you," Martin said, but he stood up and started to take off his gear. He remembered the knife beneath his chest protector and left it on. "Fine, let's go."

Jorge led him through the clubhouse, past the manager's offices, and to an elevator. He hit the "Up" arrow and keyed the fourth floor when they stepped into the elevator. On the ride up, Martin could smell a sour stink coming off his manager. Fear sweat. He probably reeked of it, too.

The elevator doors opened on what looked like a typical cubicle farm. Bright fluorescent lights illuminated a maze of beige walls and beige desks. A row of offices ran along the far wall, glass doors with the names of important people stenciled on them. All were dark except one, and it was there Jorge led him.

The Stars' manager knocked on the door, and a voice answered. "Come in." The voice was even, cultured, and the subtle hint of a British accent lingered over a few syllables.

Jorge opened the door to a well-appointed office complete with a big mahogany desk, two leather chairs, an antique brass bar cart, and a bank of windows overlooking the empty field below. Behind the desk sat a man dressed in an expensive-looking, charcoal gray suit, with a white shirt and black tie beneath. His face was handsome but cold, with a hawkish nose, bright blue eyes, and full lips. He looked to be in his early fifties, but not a trace of gray marred his ink-black hair.

"Ah, Mister Wagner," the man said. Not Martin or Wags. Mr. Wagner. No one called him that unless they were collecting money or trying to sell him something. "Please, come in and sit down." The man gestured at one of the chairs in front of the desk, then glanced at Jorge, his lips quirking in a slight frown. "Thank you, Mister Vasquez. I can take it from here."

Jorge, looking quite relieved to be dismissed, left the room and shut the door.

Martin was familiar with most of the Giants' brass, but he'd never seen this man before. "So, who are you?"

"My name is Isaac Harker," the man said. "I am a special assistant to General Manager Frank Wallace."

That name Martin did know. Frank Wallace was not only the General Manager for the big club, but he also had a sizable ownership stake in the team. The mention of the GM and Mr. Harker's position convinced Martin to sit gingerly in one of the leather chairs, trying not to wince as his right knee voiced its extreme displeasure at the movement.

"Knees?" Harker said, smiling. It was not a friendly smile.

"Yeah, I'm a thirty-seven-year-old catcher. My fucking knees hurt," Martin said. "Now, why are we talking?"

"To the point." Harker smiled. "Fair enough." He opened a drawer and pulled out a plain manilla folder. He pushed it toward Martin. "The Giants would like to offer you a new contract."

That caught Martin completely off guard. "I—I don't understand."

"Turn to the last page," Harker said and steepled his fingers in front of his mouth, hiding his expression.

Martin opened the folder. Inside was a short stack of papers held together with a binder clip, a new contract. He flipped to the signature page, which also summarized the Giants' offer. At first, he thought he'd misread the number printed there. Over-the-hill catchers didn't get three-year, eight-figure contracts. Martin opened his mouth, trying to force out words. None came.

"I hope that number is sufficient," Mr. Harker said. "Your agent believed it was."

Martin hadn't spoken to Hannah Grier in six months. His agent had stopped returning his calls ever since he'd been kicked down to Triple-A. "Why?"

"Simple. Andrei Dinescu will be called up to the Giants in two weeks," Harker said. "The organization would very much like his personal catcher to accompany him."

Sudden, awful fear gripped Martin. "Are you insane? After what happened tonight?"

"I watched the game from here, Mister Wagner. I saw a remarkable display of talent and an even more remarkable display of leadership and control, by you."

"Control?" Martin barked laughter. "He almost killed me, and he broke Calhoun's arm in half!"

Harker's frown returned. This was not a man accustomed to contradiction. "There is obviously room for improvement, but your presence kept the situation from getting further out of hand."

Martin sat back in his chair, stunned. "We got lucky. That's all."

"I don't believe in luck," Harker said. "I believe in science; I believe in people, and I believe Andrei Dinescu will lead the Giants to another World Series."

Martin leaned forward, his chest protector creaking. "What exactly do you do for Frank Wallace?" The position of special assistant to the GM could mean just about anything; it often allowed a general manager to hire people with specialties outside of traditional baseball operations.

Harker smiled, wider this time. His teeth were an ugly shade of yellow. Not a smoker's stain, something different. They showed age that his face did not. "My duties are varied, but for the most part, I serve Mister Wallace as a scout."

"You found Andrei," Martin said.

"Yes, among other…uniquely gifted individuals," Harker replied. "Andrei is the most seasoned of my recent acquisitions, as you have seen."

"I've seen a tormented young man with a condition I can't begin to understand put in a situation where he and others are likely to be hurt or killed," Martin said flatly.

"Tell me, Mister Wagner," Harker said. "Describe Mister Dinescu's performance tonight only in terms of baseball." Martin opened his mouth to protest, but Harker held up one hand, an imperious gesture. "Indulge me."

"No one could touch him," Martin said grudgingly. "I've never seen anyone throw that hard and with that much control. He's unhittable."

"His fastball has been clocked at one hundred and thirteen miles per hour," Harker said. "When the moon is full. As you have no doubt witnessed, his performance waxes and wanes with the phases of that bright satellite."

Martin was still trying to wrap his head around 113 miles per hour. The fastest pitch ever recorded was 105, and Andrei had blown past that. "Yeah, but he's pretty useless two weeks out of the month. How is that going to work?"

"Is there some rule that states a team *must* pitch its starters every five days?" Harker said. "Could a team not pitch its best every day if they so choose? Such was the case in the early days of the game."

"That's not exactly the kind of thing you can hide," Martin said. "What are you going to tell the media, other teams?" He grimaced when he realized Harker had led him ever so gently into a trap. He was thinking more about how to explain Andrei's abilities than serving as a caretaker for a monster.

"There are so many stories we could tell them, but in the end, when Andrei is good for five or six victories each month when his abilities are at their highest, who would argue?"

"And if he loses control and eats one of the opposing players?"

Harker's lips curled in an ugly sneer. "We have taken steps to control such vulgar urges. A simple poultice of wolfsbane keeps his transformation under control while allowing him access to most of his physical gifts."

"The rosin bag," Martin said.

Harker nodded and pointed at Martin's chest. "In addition, the talisman you wear is inscribed with the image of Saint Ailbe and is quite rare and powerful, as you saw tonight."

Martin could not deny that these tricks or magic or whatever they were had been effective, and the contract sitting unsigned before him represented something he'd thought only a pipe dream. The money would allow him to pay his debts, retire, and a small unwelcome voice in the back of his head also reminded him his doctor had threatened to stop prescribing Percocet and procuring it elsewhere would be expensive.

"Plus, as I have said, you and the boy have a bond," Harker continued. "That much is clear."

"What if I say no?" Martin asked, though he felt nauseous at the thought of turning away from this opportunity.

"Then you will receive your unconditional release from the Stars, and you will never play professional baseball again," Harker said with a shrug. It wasn't a threat, just a simple fact. His next words, on the other hand, were definitely a threat. "And should you speak to anyone about

Andrei's true nature, considerable and terrible resources will be levied against you and all those you care about."

Martin swallowed, remembering the hulking trainer who had come out to collect Andrei. He thought about Steph's conspicuous absence as well, and about how he definitely cared for her.

Harker shook his head and sighed. "I loathe threats. They are uncivilized and unnecessary when evidence is so much more convincing." He opened his desk drawer again and removed another folder, slimmer than the one that held Martin's new contract. He set it on his desk and placed one long-fingered hand atop it. "What do you know about Andrei's background? Has he told you anything?"

"I don't know anything other than where he came from?" Martin said. "The kid isn't exactly a chatterbox."

"Yes, well, that is somewhat understandable. His story is a tragic one, sadly. For example, the village where we found Andrei in Moldova had been experiencing a series of horrific murders." Harker paused and looked pointedly at Martin. "We covered them up, of course. Money can purchase many things in that part of the world, especially silence."

Fear and nausea mixed in Martin's belly, and he wiped at his mouth. He knew what was coming, an ugly truth he had long suspected and patently ignored.

Harker opened the file. It was full of photos. Like crime scene photos, glaring with splashes of crimson and pale flesh. "His sister," Harker said, pushing one of the photos at Martin.

Martin swallowed and forced himself to look. The

girl in the photo was probably about fifteen, but it was hard to tell since most of her face had been torn off. She lay on her back in a small bedroom, exposed teeth gleaming bone-white from the wet ruin of her face. There was so much blood. It splashed the walls in gaudy streaks and fanned out like gruesome angel wings beneath the body. "Jesus…"

Harker slid another photo across the desk. "His father."

Andrei's father had clearly tried to defend himself. His arms were crossed over his face, and huge chunks of flesh were missing from them. His belly had been torn open and the entrails pulled out in fat, pink ropes. An acid squirt of bile rose up Martin's throat.

Harker went to pull another photo, and Martin held up his hand. "Stop. No more."

The Giants' special assistant to the GM calmly picked up the photos he'd shown Martin and put them back in the file. He did not return the folder to the drawer.

"Does he know?" Martin asked.

Harker shook his head. "When he's under the thrall of the moon, when he transforms fully, he has no memory of the time he spends as the beast. A mercy, I suppose, but more likely a way for the curse to continue. Any sane person would end their own lives if they *knew* they were responsible for such atrocities."

"But he still has to ask about his family, right?" Martin said. The weight of simply knowing Andrei's terrible secret settled over him like a leaden shroud.

"Of course, he does, but we've seen to that," Harker replied. "The rest of his family has been paid handsomely to stay silent on that matter and to avoid unapproved communications with Andrei."

"How can you do this to him?" Martin said. "It's… it's monstrous."

Harker snorted. "Monstrous, you say? What is the alternative? We tell him he has murdered half his family, at which point he will refuse to play baseball. That we cannot have. To be blunt, Mister Wagner, if he does not play baseball for the San Francisco Giants under controlled conditions, we must ensure he can never be a threat to anyone. Do you understand?"

Martin did, and a tiny voice in the back of his mind wondered aloud if that wouldn't be best for everyone. He silenced it. "Yeah, I get it."

"We can control him to some degree, but you were chosen because we thought the boy would take to you, consider you a trusted ally, even a friend. Someone who could help him control the worst of his…urges."

"What exactly are you asking me to do?" He knew the answer, but he couldn't admit it to himself quite yet.

"Simple. You and I work together to further ameliorate any potential dangers that remain." Harker tapped the file with one finger. "Your influence on the boy could help prevent something like this from happening again. That said, even if you refuse my offer, Andrei Dinescu *will* pitch in the major leagues."

"And then if he goes full postal, it's my fault, huh?" Martin said and swallowed. It was the same pitch Jorge had used. Harker's was simply blunter and more terrifying.

Harker shrugged. "Your words, but with all I've told

and shown you, I am inclined to agree some fault might be yours to shoulder."

Martin sat back in his chair, looking at the unsigned contract in front of him. His choice was either refuse to sign it, leave everything he'd ever known, become destitute, and maybe, on some future date, watch Andrei Dinescu murder a dozen ballplayers live on ESPN. Or sign the contract, make more money than he'd ever dreamed of, control the situation (or at least have the illusion of control), and retire in three years with his morality mostly intact. The decision was ugly, painful, and easy. "You got a pen?"

Harker's jaundiced smile returned, and he pulled an ornate brass pen from his jacket. He handed it over.

Martin signed the contract. Now it was his turn to make some noise. "I have a question for you."

"Please ask," Harker said magnanimously.

"Is everyone who knows about Andrei on board with this little venture?"

Harker nodded. "I can assure you all members of the Giants in the know, from top to bottom, are in full support."

"Uh-huh," Martin said, reaching inside his chest protector and pulling the silver knife free. He tossed it onto the desk, and it made a weighty clunking sound. "Then why did this show up in my locker right before the game?"

Harker's nostrils flared as if he'd just smelled something particularly rotten.

"It's silver," Martin said.

"I know what it is, Mister Wagner," Harker said, his

voice rising just enough to let Martin know he'd poked a tiny hole in the man's icy composure. "You had this with you during the game?"

"I did. Almost used it, too," Martin admitted. "So, yeah, I'll go along with this, I'll do what I can to, uh, ameliorate the situation, but I don't believe for one fucking second you've considered all the variables in this shit show you're about to attempt."

Harker swept the knife off the desk and into a drawer, which he shut, then locked. "You've made your point, Mister Wagner. Our preparations may not be entirely sufficient. I shall endeavor to improve them. I don't suppose you have any idea who might have put the knife in your locker?"

"I don't," Martin said and hoped whoever it was had gotten the fuck out of town before those considerable and terrible resources Harker had mentioned could be brought to bear. A chilling thought rose to the surface of his mind, and Steph's absence on the field tonight made a terrible kind of sense. *God, Steph. These are not people you want to fuck around with.*

Harker reached across the desk and retrieved the signed contract. "Your agent will forward you a copy," he said, then stood. "Our business is concluded." He did not offer his hand.

"For the moment," Martin agreed. He got up and left the office. His knees sent little stabs of agony up and down his legs while his brain sent little stabs of guilt straight into his heart.

May 28ᵗʰ

Martin figured that Steph had to know what he'd done because it took her two full days to return his many frantic voicemails and texts. When she finally answered her phone, her voice was strained, though she sounded more tired than pissed.

"What do you want, Martin?"

"What do I want?" he said. "How the hell can you ask that? I want to know you're okay. I want to talk about what happened on the field the other night...and before that."

"Any chance you want to talk about the deal you signed with the Giants?" she said, the venom in her tone practically burning his ear.

Fuck. He'd hoped to break that to her in person. "Uh, how did you know about that?" he said lamely.

"The Stars are on the road, and you're not. Plus, they called up another pitcher and a catcher from San Jose to fill the roster spots. Doesn't take a genius to figure that one out."

"Okay, fine, you're not wrong, but I need to talk to you, and what I have to say shouldn't be said over the phone. Please."

Silence for a long, aching moment, and then, "I'll meet you at Grady's in an hour."

"Okay. Steph, I'm sor—"

The line went dead.

Grady's was one of those places that looked like it should have gone out of business years ago but somehow clung to life from a trickle of business brought in by a small subset of customers. In this case, that was Sacramento Stars ballplayers and their friends, and it provided the owners of Grady's Tavern with enough income to keep the place operating and relatively clean. Relatively being the operative word. The wood floors were dingy and gouged with cleat marks—Martin knew more than a few players didn't change out of their uniforms to grab a quick drink. The scent of old beer mixed with a slight fart smell of the inedible hotdogs they used to serve hung in the air. The lighting was just a shade up from dungeon-like, and the tables and chairs scattered haphazardly in front of the bar looked like they'd been selected at random from a dozen thrift stores. Probably because they had.

Grady's served only the cheapest American shit water: Bud Light, Miller High Life, Pabst Blue Ribbon. They even had the extremely low-rent Keystone on tap, something Martin had never seen before or since.

When Martin walked in, Farley, the rotund, mutton-chopped bartender and part-time bouncer, tipped him a wave. Martin wasn't exactly a regular, but he'd had his share of bad beer and stale pretzels in the dark confines of Grady's Tavern.

Steph was already there and had selected a table as far from the bar as possible, near the ancient, grime-encrusted jukebox, which was playing something twangy and awful. Smart. The distance and noise from the juke would cover their conversation. Not that there was anyone to hear it.

With the Stars out of town, they had the bar to themselves.

Martin had put on his best jeans and a clean, white button-up shirt for the meeting. It was a mistake. Steph was in yoga pants and an oversized t-shirt. There were heavy bags under her eyes, and the frown lines around her mouth were canyon deep. She looked like she hadn't slept in days. She looked scared, and she looked absolutely pissed. A half-empty pitcher of flat beer, looking for all the world like urine, sat in front of the Stars' strength and conditioning coach.

Steph looked up at him and frowned. "Why are you all gussied up?"

"I, uh...um...I don't know," Martin stammered. What had he been thinking? That this was some kind of fucking date? His cheeks burned as he pulled out the other chair and sat.

"When do you and Andrei leave?" Steph asked and reached for the pitcher. She filled her mug but did not offer the second empty glass to Martin.

"Erm, the thirty-first," Martin replied.

"What did they offer you?" Steph took a sip of her beer, grimaced, and settled back in her chair. Her eyes were hard and flinty, and they bored directly into Martin's soul.

"Is that really important?"

"What the *fuck* did they offer you, Martin?" Steph said, almost spitting the words.

"Three years, fifteen million," he said. Words that had once thrilled him fell from his mouth like dead birds.

"Not bad," Steph said. "Hard to turn down. Did they make you sign the contract in blood?"

"Look, I didn't have a choice," Martin said, trying not

to sound defensive and failing. "If I didn't sign, they would've released me, and I'd never play ball again."

"Would that be so bad? You're a catcher a stone's throw from forty with fucked-up knees, so maybe that's the way it should be," Steph said, her tone softening. "It's the natural order of things. What you're doing now is not natural at all, and you know it."

"I can control him," Martin said more forcefully, because part of him actually believed that. "I can keep him from hurting anyone."

"And keep drawing that millionaire's paycheck." She laughed bitterly.

That pissed him off. "Hey, can we stop pretending like I'm not putting myself at considerable fucking risk here. He's a goddamn—" He stopped short.

"Go on," she said. "I want to hear you say it."

He couldn't. It was still too fantastical, too absurd, however true he knew it to be. "He's a scared kid with a power he doesn't understand or deserve. He's not a monster." Those horrific photos Harker had shown him said otherwise, but he'd come too far down this path to turn back.

Steph looked away, her eyes reddening, tears standing at the corners. "I'm not pretending you're not in danger, asshole. That's why I'm so pissed at you. That's why I put that dagger in your locker. I wanted to give you a way out."

His breath caught in his throat, and he desperately wished he had a drink to wash down the seething doubt and guilt. "I know what I'm doing," he said. It felt like the most blatant lie in the world.

"You don't. You can't. I know what happened on that field, what he almost became, what he almost did," she said. "He's going to kill someone. Maybe it'll be you. I hope to God not, but it'll happen."

Part of him wanted to tell her what Harker had shared with him just so he wouldn't have to carry that awful burden by himself, but that was selfish and stupid and would only put her in more danger. "Look, Steph, you've made it clear you think I'm making a mistake, but I met one of the guys running the show for the Giants, and he's more monster than Andrei could ever be."

"He the same one that offered you the contract?" The accusation was naked and laced with disgust.

"Yes, and he knows about the knife, but I didn't tell him who put it there."

She took another sip of beer. "So, what are you saying?"

"I'm saying they'll find out, and they'll do more than fire you. These people think they can game the system with people like Andrei, win world championships and make shit tons of money doing it. They will keep their dirty laundry secret any way possible."

"So what am I supposed to do, Martin? I make sixty thousand dollars a year; I have no savings, no family, and no options. If they come after me, there's not much I can do about it."

Martin took a deep breath. This was going to be the hard part. Harder than saying goodbye, harder than the naked, ugly truth she'd exposed about his decision. He pulled a folded envelope from his back pocket. He put it on the table between them. "I drained my savings and sold the 'vette."

She eyed the envelope like a poisonous snake. "What the fuck is that?"

"It's a cashier's check for one hundred and eighty thousand dollars," he said. "Enough for you to leave and start over somewhere. I'll send you more when I can."

"Fuck you, Martin," Steph said, her lips quivering. "You think you can buy your way out of this?"

He shook his head. "I just want you to be safe."

"You want me to be safe?" she said, and her face changed, the expression of rage and betrayal giving way to a sad smile, and behind that, the faint glimmer of hope. "Then come with me. Let's take this envelope and leave Sacramento, leave California. We can hook on to some independent team in the middle of nowhere, make enough to survive."

"What are you saying? What about…"

"He doesn't exist. I lied. I don't know why. Maybe because after the last time we were together, I felt something I haven't felt in a long time." She stared down at her beer. "It scared me."

"Why didn't you tell me?" Here was the one thing that might have made him reject Harker's offer, and they both knew it was too late.

She wiped her eyes. "I don't know. I don't know."

He drew in a shuddering breath. "I can't."

She reached across the table to take his hand, and he moved it back. "Why?"

"Because you're right. He might kill someone, and I might be able to stop it."

Steph stared at him for a long time. Her eyes were unreadable. He searched for something to say but couldn't find any words. Finally, she stood, picked up the envelope, and left. No farewell. No, "Eat shit and die." Just an end.

May 31st

Martin had flown on a chartered jet when he'd played in the big leagues, but the Learjet sitting on the tarmac of McClellan Airport offered luxury only reserved for the elite. It would fly him to San Francisco, where he would join the Giants and begin his stint on paper as a back-up catcher and his decidedly not-on-paper stint as the caretaker to a monster.

He'd tried calling Steph a few times in the last couple of days, hating how things had ended between them, and each time it rolled to voicemail. He hoped to God she was avoiding his calls somewhere in the middle of nowhere. Somewhere without baseball. Somewhere Harker and all those vast and terrible resources he mentioned wouldn't think to look.

He'd showed Harker the silver knife Steph had put in his locker for leverage against the man, and it had worked. It had also hurt the one person he really cared about. He felt nauseous, but the contract was signed, his fate sealed.

When he stepped aboard the plane, Martin was surprised to see Andrei sitting near the back, nestled in one of the plush leather seats. He hadn't seen the pitcher since his near-disastrous start almost a week ago. Also on the plane was the thuggish trainer who had escorted Andrei from the field that night. His name, Martin had learned through Harker, was Oleg Danov, and though he did seem to have the skills of a strength and conditioning coach, it was made clear he had *other* skills to deal with what Harker had termed "a worst-case scenario."

Martin made his way down the aisle, ignoring Oleg, and sat next to Andrei. The kid looked up and offered Martin a shy smile. He still had a slightly feral look about him, but it was more controlled. He could probably throw in the mid-nineties.

"How are you, kid?" Martin said.

"I am good," Andrei replied, then his face fell. "I...I wanted to tell you that I would not have hurt you."

Martin had heard people tell themselves all kinds of lies over the years, mostly pitchers trying to convince their managers they had enough juice for one more hitter. Andrei sounded about as convincing, but Martin appreciated the sentiment. "Hey, let's not worry about the past." He smiled. "We're going to the big leagues, man."

That didn't have the effect Martin had hoped for, and Andrei looked at the floor, his black hair flopping in front of his face. "So many people watching."

Martin put a hand on Andrei's shoulder. The muscles there still felt like coiled steel. "Don't do that. We got through your last start, and now that I'm, uh, aware of your condition, it's gonna be a cakewalk from here on out." Lying to himself came easier.

"You think?" Andrei said, desperately hopeful.

Martin had a whole kit of supplies to keep Andrei's

condition under wraps, and he was intimately familiar with the phases of the moon thanks to his very own copy of the *Old Farmer's Almanac*. "Throw strikes. That's all you need to worry about. You let me handle that other stuff."

Andrei let out a deep sigh of relief and looked up at Martin, grateful tears brimming in his eyes. "Back in my village, I had no one to help me. No one to understand—"

Martin squeezed Andrei's shoulder to comfort him, but mostly to quiet him. He didn't want to think of what had happened in Andrei's village. Couldn't think about that. Especially now. "The past, remember? We're not doing that. Okay?"

"Okay," Andrei replied.

"We're partners. I'm gonna watch your back. You're gonna watch mine," Martin said. That part was true. Harker had them both by the short hairs to some degree, and the more united they were, the less the special assistant to the GM could fuck with them.

"Yes, partners," Andrei said with a wide grin. *My, what big teeth you have.* "I like this."

Martin eyed Oleg sitting a few rows ahead of them. The man was listening to their conversation and would dutifully report it to Harker. Martin smiled. That was fine. Neither Oleg nor Harker were in possession of all the facts.

They didn't know Martin's knees hadn't hurt since the day after the game with the Halos and that he'd flushed all his Percocet down the toilet. He didn't need it anymore. They also didn't know about the two-inch-long scratch he'd found on his back in the shower the next morning, one which had already healed into a new scar.

ABOUT THE AUTHOR

Aeryn Rudel is a writer from Tacoma, Washington. He is the author of the Acts of War novels published by Privateer Press, and his short fiction has appeared in *Dark Matter Magazine*, *On Spec*, and *Pseudopod*, among others. He recently released the flash fiction collection *Night Walk & Other Dark Paths* with The Molotov Cocktail. Aeryn is a passionate dinosaur nerd, a baseball fanatic, and knows far more about swords than is healthy or socially acceptable. Learn more about his work at www.rejectomancy.com or on Twitter @Aeryn-Rudel.

For more howling good fun, be sure to
check out…

TOOTH & CLAW

Prologue

He ran, earth-pounding, heart-pumping, and head-long. About him, the dense woodlands provided no respite; the monsters chasing him had the advantage, the die forever cast in their favor. He could hear them now in the distance, the whoops and screams of delight, the blood-lust making them confident and weakening his resolve.

How the hell had it come to this? Where had it all gone so wrong? He wasn't a bad person; he worked as a medic, for Christ's sake. A third of his thirty-five years on this earth had been devoted to caring for and saving the lives of others. In fact, his last memory was leaving St. Norman's General Hospital after a twelve-hour shift. He recalled heading to his car, a second-hand Honda Civic. Then someone had stepped from the shadows and every cell in his body wanted to explode as the crackle of a taser sliced through the air.

He'd woken god-knows-how-much-time later, dazed and caged. A monotone voice through the Tannoy system in the plasterboard ceiling had told him the deal. He'd be released from the cage. All he had to do to earn his freedom was evade capture. The question as to why he'd been chosen was always at the back of his mind, but survival instinct took charge as soon as he was blindfolded by two thickset security guards. They had ignored his pleas and questions, threatening instead that he would get the taser again if he didn't *shut the fuck up.*

He was dumped in woodlands, told to wait five minutes before removing the hood. It wasn't a request.

Now he was running for his life. No cliché, no adage, just total and utter fact. The terrain proved a treacherous obstacle of low branches cutting into his face and thorny bushes tearing at his clothing and the exposed flesh of his hands.

An embankment loomed ahead, the embodiment of his current dilemma. He went low, digging his hands into the undergrowth, using the foliage to drag his ex-hausted body to the brow, spurred on by the thought that he might actually find a way out.

There was a dull thud, and the ground next to his head exploded in a plume of dirt and leaves. He cried out in surprise, climbing to his feet, lurching, then falling forward to all fours, scampering up the incline like a proverbial scared rabbit.

There came another dull thud and a momentary sharp, searing pain in his lower back. His severed spinal cord took pity on him and robbed him of all feeling below his waist. His legs collapsed, and he rolled down the embankment, crashing through the bracken until he lay on the woodland floor. He watched the two men emerge from the nearby bushes, shouldering suppressed hunting rifles as they came. Their night vision goggles made them appear more inhuman than their actions.

There was resignation that his final moments were playing out. Confirmation came when one of the men pulled a serrated hunting knife from his belt, stooped, and cut his throat.

The two men watched their prey bleed out, life draining from his eyes.

"Man, don't you just *love* this fucking place?" the man with the knife said.

"Damn straight," his colleague replied with a grin.

His partner smeared blood from the knife across his own sweaty brow. He offered up the blade.

The other man shook his head. "Your kill, your honor."

"Okay, boss."

As one man sheathed the knife, the other pulled out his cell phone from his green windbreaker, activating it with a single touch of his thumb. The line kicked in, and he spoke with barely suppressed excitement.

"We're ready for the next one."

Chapter One

The spruce trees created a jagged edge to the skyline, above which the incoming chopper was a mere smudge against the gray clouds. The thick staccato of rotor blades rolled across the valley, and the landscape below wavered as foliage succumbed to the caress of the breeze coming in from the southwest.

The undulating countryside leveled off, giving way to a huge lawn, and perched on the edge of beautifully rich, manicured grass was Cofton Grange, its quarter turrets and yellowed sandstone still glimmering in the fading light.

The stately home was built in 1709 on the site of Brunswick Hall, an equally grand building that had become a victim of canon-fire in 1645, at the height of the English Civil War. Before its demolition, Brunswick Hall had a reputation for attracting controversial figures. There were rumors that several key members of the Gunpowder Plot had stayed in its halls during the original planning stages, and its spurious amity had extended to hosting a dinner for Matthew Hopkins, the notorious Witchfinder General when he passed through the lands.

When The Grange was built, it continued with its tradition of associations with the shadowy side of society. Highwayman Dick Turpin held up three coaches on nearby roads, and Sally Salisbury, a notorious celebrity prostitute, allegedly frequented parties before her imprisonment in 1723. During the first 100 years, The Grange had seen both the French and American revolutions, unprecedented stability of the Ottoman Empire, and the publication of *Gulliver's Travels* and *Robinson Crusoe*. For the locale, it was a constant entity, as was the twelve-hundred acres of hills and woodlands that made up its estate.

Another constant was the man who watched the inbound chopper with eyes the color of gray marble. Just like the grand building rising up behind him, Jacob Rothschild's refined exterior was a facade that hid an ugly and controversial past. He was mild-mannered and soft spoken. His eyes were cupped in heavy lids, and his cheeks were high and angular. Although he had a slight frame and fell two inches short of six feet, his presence commanded attention the way a head teacher's silent poise quells a hall of rowdy kids.

Albert Rothschild, Jacob's father, had also commanded authority. But his presentation—his means—of getting things done was perhaps not as refined, not as polished, as those adopted by his son in the years that were to come.

That was not to say Jacob was averse to extreme prejudice; on occasion, it was a necessary part of his business. But his father used violence as a tool to send a very clear message to those reluctant to play ball. For Jacob, it was about keeping people *quiet*.

His father was an effective criminal but lacked vision. He didn't see anything beyond money and providing for his family. Jacob understood the perverse nobility of fatherhood and the responsibilities that came with such a role. The fact he had not sought to have a family was a testament to the belief that grand success and the shackles of family life simply did not mix. Either way, when his father was gunned down in a pub in Birmingham as he ate pie and cheese-mash, Jacob and his mother had to get savvy, and damn quick. When their crime empire appeared vulnerable, Jacob was twenty-one years old and had his own portfolio, underworld property (mainly safe houses for those on the run), and trafficking anything that could be crammed into cramped spaces. It was a modest business, but once he siphoned his father's assets into it and they got the hell out of town, the whole thing grew beyond profitable. By the time he'd acquired The Grange, his personal assets were estimated at over 1.5 billion.

All of it squeaky-clean.

At the point where he took on The Grange, the commercial and physical integrity of the estate was in dire straits: the building run down and the grounds neglected after being poorly managed by Lord Atwitch, a third-rate businessman with a bought title.

During the acquisition, Rothschild had agreed to be a

silent partner to bring the house and grounds back to their former glory. But his motivation was not about gaining privilege or titles; it was about hiding in plain sight. Yes, the thought the house had a history of assumed notoriety did give it a whimsical attraction, but Rothschild was above all of that because there was no doubt from anyone who knew him that he was an exceptionally good criminal.

In the first eight years of renovating The Grange and its bank balance, he had taken over responsibility for Grange Holdings PLC, the company created with the intention of bringing the building back to its glory days. After ten years, the entire estate belonged to him, the previous owner having sold over the deeds shortly before "disappearing abroad." In truth, Lord and Lady Atwitch were strangled and dismembered while on holiday in the US before their carcasses became a special treat for the guests at an alligator farm in Louisiana. Just like the nefarious affairs of The Grange itself, this rumor had no evidence to support it.

Over the next twenty years, Rothschild and his mother turned The Grange into a prosperous and thriving estate, generating a place tourists and top-end pleasure seekers alike clamored to visit. And visit they did, in droves; business was thriving, with so many people and so much money changing hands.

But success was a cloak behind which the real industry thrived. And that industry was, of course, crime. Top-end, high-stakes crime.

Over time, Jacob had become as successful as he

was secretive, and these two facets were intrinsic, a synergy that maintained his prestige. His mother had died only two years ago, in one of the rooms at The Grange, a team of care-givers making sure her end came with both comfort and dignity. It was the first and last time for many years Jacob could remember crying. Not in public, of course. At the funeral (she'd been interned in the family mausoleum deep in the woods), he'd been stoic and refined, the persona he wore as well as his suit. Later, in his chambers, he'd allowed the tears to fall.

He relished the grief, knowing that his long-suffering mother deserved every single tear he'd shed for her. Without this gentle and unassuming woman in his life, his primary focus had become his business interests.

Jacob's focus at that moment, however, was the H155 heading toward him. The helipad was twenty meters away, a raised concrete plinth with a short run of steps down to a wide gravel path. As well as the approaching chopper, he was also mindful of the events that had been planned for the coming evening. It was a special time for special people, exceptional people that operated beyond the realms of the humble commoner. Though he'd never admit it to anyone else, Jacob didn't think it was too conceited to consider the events laid out were even above kings and queens themselves.

Yes, some things could be bought with money. But not everything.

Nature had a price list all of its own.

The helicopter made three trips and brought a guest list of four people. As each passenger disembarked, Jacob greeted them. Standing at his side was Sanders—a waiter dressed in a smart white tunic and starched black trousers—who carried a flute of iced champagne on a small, silver serving tray.

In his mid-thirties, Sanders had striking blue eyes and a neatly trimmed beard. He was immediately attentive to the guests as each disembarked, and he escorted them to their rooms on the third floor with a confident air.

As he walked, Sanders paid careful attention to each of them, his face scrutinizing every move, every nuance. Each of the guests considered this a sign of his time and expertise in service.

They could not have been more wrong.

In one of the guestrooms, Martin "Marty" Woodhead placed his travel bag on the edge of the huge four-poster bed. The headboard was made from Blackwood, carved with intricate two-dimensional images of peacocks with tail plumage extended like great, ornate fans.

Marty sat on the mattress as he took in the room, his feet bumping against the valance. The guest room was large, and the floors were covered in plush carpet and thick, expensive-looking rugs that were vibrant, as though they had been bought that very day. The walls, covered in heavy wallpaper, had garish patterns, and heavy drapes hung like burgundy sentinels to either side of the high, leaded windows. The furniture was old, each sideboard or small table warped and pitted by age, but the surfaces gleamed with lacquer and varnish. He sniffed and gave out a small sneeze, dust and the smell of wood heavy in the air.

He shuffled forward so that his backside was almost sliding off of the bed; only then could he plant his feet on the floor. He dug his heavy boots into the carpets, enjoying the way the pile gave way under his soles like he was walking through lush, green grass.

Marty sighed.

He was a small man with big issues. To anyone who ever asked the question, he'd say he had no truck with being five feet-four inches tall. Inside, however, his mind would play out how he could gleefully gut the inquisitor without thought. Instead, he would pull his bearded lips into a casual smile, his deep brown eyes twinkling with mischief.

Over the years, he'd compensated for his lack of stature but building up his physical prowess. He boasted a black belt in karate, could bench press two-hundred-and-fifteen pounds, and had completed three Iron Man challenges.

As he thought about what had brought him to The Grange that evening, he pawed at his foppish fringe, brushing strands of dirty gray-blond hair from his brow. It was a nervous trait he'd inherited from his mother. Over the years, she'd used it as a ploy to distract his moronic father from doling out another beating to Marty for being "so fucking weak."

Ultimately, the bruises were the mark of his father's embarrassment. After each beating, Marty would head out to woods to nurse his contusions and displace his revenge on the wildlife there. The first time he'd killed an animal and imagined it as his father was when he only twelve years old. His father had cuffed him across the face for "backtalk," splitting Marty's lower lip, the sting and swelling immediate as he ran sobbing from the house.

Broadacre Woods was over seventy yards from their home, ten acres of green belt land overseen by the National Trust. The site was a favorite with local ramblers and kids out on their Duke of Edinburgh Award schemes, but no matter what the reason people came to Broadacre, its tranquility soothed all souls.

For a time, it had certainly been anesthetic to Marty's domestic injuries from his father's rogue temper. In that summer of 1977, hiding in the foliage of Broadacre, quiet sobs sending shudders through his body, Marty spat blood from his battered lips and wished his father dead. The thought was bright and came with guilt, the latter emotion strong but not enough to be outshone by his primordial need to get even.

His breath came in short gasps, the quiet rage building. Then he'd heard the sound, a rustling in the undergrowth that stalled the breath in his throat and made his head swim, his heart suddenly ice-water in his chest. The rabbit had crawled from a bush moments later, its ears flat to its back, a hind leg trailing behind it. They were kindred spirits in that moment, two wounded souls seeking solace under the canopy of trees.

Unlike Marty, the injured rabbit was not quiet in its suffering; it gave out tiny squeals each time it moved. The animal's pain and fear became a focal point in the very second Marty's anger toward his abusive father was at its peak. He'd reached for the rabbit and broke its neck with a single twist of its head, but in his mind he wasn't putting an ailing creature out of its misery; he was snapping the neck of his own father, and the surge of power this act gave him was a dizzying sense of liberty he'd never experienced before.

Seconds later, with the rabbit limp in his hand, Marty had begun making plans to murder his father. And several years later, he'd almost succeeded.

The telephone on the cupboard next to the bed rang, startling him from his murky thoughts.

"Mister Woodhead," Jacob said into his ear. "It is time for aperitifs in The Seaton Suite."

The phone went dead before he could respond. Rubbing his brow, Marty made for the *en suite* to wash up. Within ten minutes, he was making his way downstairs, thoughts now turned to the excitement the rest of the evening promised.

The ballroom of Cofton Grange was situated on the ground floor, accessed by a wide corridor to the left of a sweeping stone staircase central to the main hall. The ballroom was a place of high white walls and deep cornices. Blanched and fluted stone columns supported the lofty ceiling. Huge chandeliers hung down like glimmering beehives, the crystal giving off multiple starbursts.

The dance floor took up more than half of the room; oak boards shimmered under the bright lights. Around this area, circular tables were laid out, tablecloths turning them into white puck shapes flanked by high-backed, gilded chairs with red velvet manchettes and seats.

A bar ran the length of one wall, before which stools were placed at sociable intervals, and several feet away, a row of low cartouche tables ran parallel to the drink-ing area. At that moment, two people were perched on stools sipping vodka tonics. The bartender had served them and gone off to find more ice, and his only patrons chatted amicably, their excited voices bouncing around the walls.

Pippa and Antonia Okill sat near each other on the stools. Antonia's legs were long, her brown combat pants pinned to her trim waist with a thick leather belt, the sil-ver buckle fashioned into the head of a snarling panther. The chiffon blouse was lime green with a halter neck, and her thick, black hair fell into stark curls about her bare, pale shoulders.

"And I told him that you spell it O-K-I-L-L, and there ain't no goddamned apostrophe," Antonia was say-ing. "Man, that guy was as thick as frigging custard."

In contrast, Pippa was slightly smaller; her hair wasn't wanton. Instead, it was pulled up into a bunch and pinned with long grips that looked like tiny daggers. She wore black cargo pants and a white t-shirt. "Why can't people get our damn name right?" Pippa said with a frown. "Is it that hard?"

Antonia winked. "Well, that was the next question I asked him. I've got to say, there's a guy to go to if you ain't there for intellectual conversation."

Pippa laughed in disbelief. "You are such a whore, Antonia Okill!"

They both clung to each other as they giggled.

The Okill sisters were not sisters at all. They were, in fact, first cousins but had been raised together when Pippa's parents had been killed in a freak accident while on vacation on the coast, something to do with a high wave and a low wall, the news reports had said later. Pippa was three at the time, and her Aunt Clair and Uncle Armand, her father's brother, stepped in to raise her. At six years old, Antonia had bonded with her younger cousin, giving her support and relishing having someone else to play with in the family home. They'd become inseparable—insufferable Clair and Armand often joked—during the course of childhood, though the relationship was to become far deeper as they grew into young women, especially after a coronary snuffed Uncle Armand from the earth, leaving Aunt Clair to draw comfort from her daughters to the point of suffocation.

It was during this time the family ethic became stronger than drive and ambition. "Without family, a person has no purpose," Aunt Clair would say over her second bottle of Chablis. By the time she died of liver sclerosis three years after Armand had departed this mortal coil, Aunt Clair was on two bottles of scotch a day. She left behind not only two young, grieving women, but also debts large enough for Pippa and Antonia to be left penniless. Solace came from an unlikely place, an estranged relative they knew only as Uncle Roger, Armand's brother, who no one in the family would ever discuss, let alone invite to family gatherings. When an opportunity came to bend a few rules to make sure they would be secure forever, Uncle Roger was there offering a solution, and the sisters jumped at it.

Family was family after all.

A polite cough made them turn their heads. The barman had returned and was waiting patiently for acknowledgment.

Antonia sat upright. "Okay, you got our attention, fella. What we gotta do now, read your mind?"

If the bartender was embarrassed, there was no sign of it. "Mister Rothschild and the other guests are waiting for you in The Seaton Suite, Miss. Can I show you the way?"

He turned and headed off without waiting for a response.

Pippa slid off of her stool, eager to follow. "If that guy didn't have a broom up his ass, I think he'd be living in a bucket."

Chuckling, the women followed their stoic guide.

Oscar Jarman took a sip of his *Macallan In Lalique*, 65-year-old scotch whiskey, savoring the smooth heat in his throat and the weight of the lead crystal tumbler in his hand. The Macallan came in at just under fifty grand a bottle, the Waterford crystal tumbler around nine hundred pounds per glass. He loved the finer things in life and had always known they would come to him.

In his guestroom, he was surrounded by the kind of affluence he always felt he deserved. Refinery and gran-deur came in abundance, the furnishings lavish, and the setting oozing with history. He felt content here; he felt *at home*.

Oscar had always felt bound for greatness. His origins did not give a hint to this, a small boy born to a civil servant, his father a mysterious figure in the British consulate in Hong Kong. His mother's affair had been brief, but the responsibilities she came away with were to be life-long. No sooner had she'd made known her pregnancy, her consulate lover became very busy, meetings taking up his time from that day forward.

She got the hint after several weeks of trying to get hold of him. She'd returned from Hong Kong, back to the small mining village in The Rhonda Valley, mid-Wales, where she stayed with her parents until Oscar was born, a bastard yet still loved, supported by his mother and grand-parents.

When Oscar was six years old, he stumbled upon his

mother and grandparents having a heated discussion in the parlor of the small miner's cottage he'd called home for as long as he could recall. The argument had stopped as soon as his presence was known, his grandfather coming over to him to scoop him up in a playful hug and taking him outside into the garden, where a low hedge separated them from the rolling hills of the Rhonda Valley beyond. But Oscar's sensitive ears could hear his mother and grandmother starting up again as soon as they thought he was out of earshot.

The next day his mother began to search for secretarial work but could find nothing locally. She went further afield, determined to raise her son independent of her parents. It was only as he got old enough to understand such things as guilt and shame that Oscar realized his mother was fundamentally embarrassed by her upbringing. When she found work across the English border, working as a PA for a local mental health trust, Oscar's mother began to rebuild their lives, but the foundations were laid on grandiosity and self-delusion.

What they'd lost became the mantra for what they deserved, and yearning fueled delusions of grandeur. Before long, Oscar's mother was insisting that their humble beginnings did not define them; had fate not been so cruel, they would have been schmoozing with ambassadors and ladies, lower-echelon Royalty, perhaps. Oscar absorbed her woes, and over time, it sculpted his ego, shaping his outlook on life until he believed the aspirations to be real. By the time he was in his teens, he was telling anyone prepared to listen that his absent father was an ambassador who had died in a car accident. He came up with stories that he told with conviction because, in part, he wished it so hard it became real to his very own psyche.

He became articulate and smooth, creating a persona as convincing as the lies he told. He was to become extraordinarily rich over time, but the achievement—like so many things in his life—belonged to someone else.

That someone went by the name of *Georgina Cox.*

With the thought of the woman who had made all of this possible still rattling around his head, Oscar showered and clipped his beard. Then he headed downstairs, where more of the trappings of wealth awaited him.

Just as Jacob had requested, the guests were assembled in The Seaton Suite, an elegant drawing room three doors away from the grand ballroom.

The suite was resplendent, all of the furnishings a sanguine mix of pastel blues, yellows, and white. A huge fireplace was embedded in one wall, the white marble surround was ornate and speckled with veins of gray. Above it was a huge landscape painting depicting a fox hunt, the images of riders almost caricature; the horses were disproportionate with their large bellies and small heads, the huntsmen majestic in bold colors of reds and white.

Opposite the fireplace was a large window, wooden frames painted white and opening out onto the clinical, ornate gardens. The uprights embedded in the gravel paths turned this baroque place of ferns and bushes into an eerie netherworld of jagged shadows and stark white light, the ambiance helped in part by the bloated moon hanging in the sky.

Between the fireplace and the window was a social space that spoke only of opulence. Twin Chesterfield sofas of rich, red leather sat at ninety degrees to a half-height rosewood table. On this table were three silver buckets, each with its own bottle of *1998 Dom Perignon Brut*. A squad of flutes stood at attention, a selection of delicate canapés keeping them company.

Marty and Oscar were standing, each eating canapés served by Sanders. The Okill sisters had parked themselves on a Chesterfield sofa and looked very comfortable indeed. Pippa enjoyed sipping champagne while Antonia quaffed a *Coors Light* directly from the bottle.

Since coming into the room, the group had exchanged pleasantries in muted conversation, but there was an atmosphere about them, their conversation guarded. To an outsider, it may have come across as the awkward exchange of strangers. Instead, it was the stilted banter of competitors before a great race. They all knew of each other, their names synonymous with the best in their profession. And they were the top of their field because of the very reason they had been called together.

They had no limits.

The room fell silent as the door opened and Jacob stepped in. He crossed the room, his face measured, a small smile playing on his lips. He appeared as a man who is comfortable with his surroundings.

A man who was in complete control.

Walking to the back of the nearest sofa, he placed both hands upon the smooth leather. "Good evening, ladies and gentlemen," he said in a smooth voice. "And welcome back to Cofton Grange."

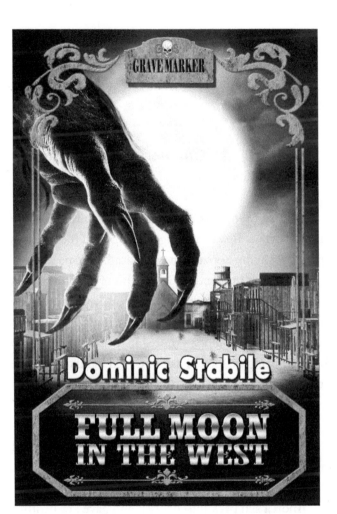

Chapter 1

Andréa Medina stopped the wagon in front of the sheriff's office. It was nearing evening, and the sun was a pink line on the horizon. Juan "Tezcat" Medina sat next to Andréa with his hands in his lap, his eyes on his soiled boots. He wore his father's tattered poncho and hat. The hat was too large for his head, and the poncho kept slipping from one shoulder. Andréa had made fun of him about it, saying he looked like a starved bandito. But the truth was he felt comforted by his father's clothing, and he was in great need of comfort.

Andréa moved to dismount, then turned to her brother. "We should speak with the sheriff, see if he has found anything."

"It is no use," Tezcat said.

Andrea slid back into her seat and gave her brother a hopeful look. "There is still time," she said.

"I cannot do it," Tezcat said. "Even if there is time, and the witch can do as she says, I cannot kill a man, much less six men."

"You can and you must."

"It is *my* wife and daughter," Tezcat said. "Why should I not let them lie in peace with God?"

Andrea's eyes widened, and she looked down at her feet a moment, considering his words. "Maria was my sister, Juana, my niece," she said, as if reaffirming her own convictions. "They are a part of me, as they are you. If you can bring them back, then that is what you must do."

Tezcat shook his head. "I should lust for revenge, but I do not." He looked at his sister. "You burn with it."

Andréa gripped his poncho and folded it back, revealing the Colt .45 on his hip. As they watched, the bullet chambers emitted a dim, purple glow that grew ever fainter, until it died.

"You brought the gun to Emygdia," she said. "Why did you accept her help if you do not want them back?"

"I do want them back," he said. "But not like this." He thought of the illusion the witch, Emygdia, had cast before the fire the night before: a dream-vision of his wife and daughter sleeping soundly, their skin glowing with life. *Bring me the souls of the six men who sent your wife and daughter across the river,* she had said, *and I will use them to bargain for your girls.*

Andréa shook her head and was about to argue further when a voice called out, "Help you two?"

Sheriff Watson stood leaning against the porch railing outside his office, smoking a cigarette. He was a white man, roughly six feet tall. He wore a full, white beard, and there was a cunning, amused quality to his expression, as if he were pulling off the greatest hoax of all time simply by standing where he was standing and wearing a star on his shirt.

"We have questions," Andréa said.

"Thought you might," Watson said, and he went back inside.

Andréa and Tezcat shared a wary glance, and then Andréa dismounted. After a moment spent watching the doorway through which Watson had just disappeared, Tezcat reluctantly followed.

Chapter 2

The Sheriff's desk was just to the left of the entrance, and behind that was a polished gun case containing a double-barrel shotgun, two Winchester repeaters, and several cartons of shells. Everything in the room, save the gun case, was covered in an even skin of dust and sand.

Sheriff Watson was standing in front of one of the two jail cells built into the back of the room, facing the man inside.

The Englishman.

Andréa and Tezcat stopped and stared at the man, unable to speak.

He was still wearing the black hat and expensive suit he'd worn the night he ordered the killing of Tezcat's wife and daughter, but some of the diamonds had left his smile. One of his blue eyes was swollen shut, and the other was as red as a bullet wound.

The Sheriff didn't turn. He stood there quietly smoking a moment, and then he said, "Caught up with him last night. I know a little about running from the Law myself, and this one's no good at it."

"I do not believe it," Andréa said.

"His friends were a sight better at fleeing, however," Watson said, ignoring her, "and I figured them to be in Mexico by now." He dropped his cigarette on the floor, stamped it out, and turned to face them. He was smiling. "But I worked our friend over anyways, just to be sure he couldn't put my mind at ease on that."

"What did he tell you?" Andréa said.

"It turns out they might have posted up somewhere nearby," Watson said, moving toward his desk and taking a seat. "Why are you so curious?"

"We are looking for them ourselves," Andréa said. "We went as far as Colina Verde, on the border, but no one has seen them."

"That so?" Watson said, smiling. He was looking at Tezcat.

"It is," Tezcat said. His voice shook, but his eyes were set firmly on the Englishman, who made a mocking sound somewhere between a laugh and a spat tooth.

"And what do you plan on doing when you find them?" Watson asked Andréa.

"What would you do?"

"I can tell you what I'll do if you and your brother decide to go vigilante," he said.

Andréa held his glare a moment, and then she turned to Tezcat. "Have you nothing to say?"

Tezcat was lost in the bloody eye of the Englishman, unconsciously playing his fingers over the butt of his pistol. He started at the mention of his name and saw that Watson and Andréa were watching him expectantly.

"I do not know if I can go through with it," he said.

The sheriff kept smiling. "What exactly are you up to?"

Tezcat had already turned back to the Englishman. He placed his hand on the butt of his gun again, trying to imagine pulling the trigger with a man on the other end of the barrel.

The sheriff observed this gesture and a gleam came into his eyes. "Heard you two rode out toward Barren Flats yesterday," he said. "You didn't happen to sit down with the witch now, did you?"

They looked at him without saying a word.

"Thought as much," Watson said, getting to his feet. "They're not God's problem yet," he said. "They got to pay my price first. They'll hang, then the good Lord can do what he pleases with them."

"We do not come with God," Andréa said.

The sheriff tensed for only a moment. "God. The Devil." He shrugged. "Makes no difference. This man and his raping, murdering friends will answer to the Law, and God and the Devil can watch." Watson sat back down and jerked his thumb toward the Englishman. "This one I'll keep close until his friends come for him, which they will."

"How do you know they will come for him?" Andréa asked.

"Turns out he's their leader."

Andréa looked at the Englishman and said, "What is a fop like you doing out here playing outlaw?"

"Playing?" the Englishman said. His calm voice was incongruous with his shattered face. "I'm not much for theatre. The fact is, I simply enjoy what I do." He nodded toward Tezcat. "Your wife, for example, was a toffer I won't soon forget. Do you know that, right before I cut her throat, she thanked me for the ride? I swear it's true."

Tezcat dropped to his knees. He had drawn his gun, but it fell from numb fingers and clattered to the floor. Andréa dropped to her knees and took her brother's face in her hands.

Watson got to his feet and marched toward the cell, taking a ring of keys from his pocket. He stood before the bars, and the Englishman rose, grinning at him. His teeth were the color of an old lemon peel.

"I warned you about running your mouth," Watson said, taking something from his pocket. At the sight of it, the Englishman scurried back to his cot. Watson opened the cell door and stood over the Englishman, who emitted a pathetic mewling sound similar to that of a wounded dog. And then Watson raised the object over his head and brought it down into the Englishman's face repeatedly until the prisoner stopped moving.

Watson backed out of the cell and locked the door. Then he went back to his desk and lit another cigarette.

Tezcat and Andréa stared at the mutilated prisoner. His face was swollen. A red gash crossed his forehead, and blood ran over his eyes. As they watched, he rose to a seated position on his cot. He drew a hand over his forehead and licked the blood from his fingers. He was in pain, but trying hard to appear as if he wasn't.

"The moon will heal my wounds," he said to Watson. "What about you, Sheriff?"

Watson took the cigarette from his mouth and exhaled smoke, as if he hadn't heard.

"The moon?" Tezcat said, feeling blood slowly flowing back into his face, his fingers. He looked at Watson. "What does he mean?" It was then he noticed the object the sheriff had used to bludgeon the prisoner. Andréa rose to her feet when she saw it as well.

A large, silver crucifix, covered in blood.

"Borrowed that from Father Lucas," Watson said. He stood, walked around his desk, and went to the window, looking out at the street.

"Like I said, I worked him over," Watson said, "and he had a story to tell. More than I wanted to hear, that's for sure. But enough so I know what I'm dealing with."

"And what is that?" Andréa said.

Watson glanced at them, and an uncharacteristic look of bashfulness crossed his face before he turned his eyes back out the window. "Skinwalkers," he said.

Chapter 3

Andréa laughed out loud. "They are bad men, and they are monsters. But they are not *MONsters*," she said.

Watson kept his eyes on the street. "They are, girl. And it makes a whole helluva lot of sense, too."

"What sense does it make?" Tezcat asked.

Watson exhaled a long breath. "You know how Doc Greely has his place out to the west of town?"

"Yes, so?" Andréa said.

"He's within spitting distance of those caves out by Briar Cliff Gorge. And he came to me one morning about a month ago looking like a man who hadn't slept a night in his life. His eyes all bloodshot, his hands shaking with sleeplessness. What was more, he was embarrassed. It took me a second to pick up on it, but once I had, I couldn't believe it. Old hard-ass Doc Greely was tip-toeing up my porch steps, hat in his hands like a boy who'd shat his pants. And when he finally spit out the words he wanted to say, I laughed. I thought he'd taken too many of his own horse-piss-and-water snake oil concoctions.

"'I've been hearing howling in the caves off my property,' he said. And when I suggested it was wolves or coyotes, he said, 'These howls did not come from anything of this world.'

"Just like that. That's when I laughed. But he just looked at me, earnest. You can tell when a man like Greely is joking because he has no aptitude for it. And you can tell when a man like Greely is telling the truth because he's not joking, and men like Greely only speak of the uncanny when they're stumbling over a bad joke or when they mean it."

Watson looked at Andréa, and then Tezcat. "And he meant it."

"You're saying this man and the men who killed my wife and daughter are Skinwalkers?" Tezcat said. His tone held the shocked disbelief he thought it should hold, but he almost believed it, looking at the prisoner, who grinned big behind those iron bars.

Watson nodded.

"How do you know?" Andréa said, pointing at the prisoner. "Because that madman said so?"

"Because I heard the howls myself," he said. "Because I tracked our friend here out to those caves last night, and caught up to him before he could slink down into the dark. I saw the tracks out there in the sand outside those caves, and I know plenty about the Indian legends regarding such creatures. I heard the howls on my way back. It was dark, and that sunset everyone's so crazy about looked like blood pooled up on the horizon. I heard the howls echoing from those caves, so loud and sharp I thought they were coming up behind me. The sound of it." He paused. Eyes narrowed, he stared out the window, his mouth working as he relived the memory. "Like men being torn apart."

Tezcat and Andréa stood silently.

Watson looked at them again. "They'll come tonight."

"How do you know?" Tezcat asked.

"Tonight starts the full moon," Watson said. "They're strongest during the full moon."

And that's when the gunshot sounded, and a bullet ripped through the window and hit Watson in the shoulder. He spun to the right and fell across his desk, sliding to the floor in a heap. Dust rose up from the floor in a cloud, and Watson gripped his shoulder and shut his eyes against the dust. He coughed, rolled, and got to his feet. He drew the .44 from his hip holster and blindly fired two rounds out the window.

Tezcat and Andréa had dropped to the floor. They stayed there a moment. Watson fell onto his backside and listened, his breath coming in heaves.

There was no return fire.

Tezcat stood up just enough to look out the window. He saw one of the Englishman's posse out there, riding back and forth on a horse, his gun drawn. Long, greasy black hair hung from a worn bucket hat. He wore a sheen of dust from his shredded duster to his mud-caked boots. Though Tezcat couldn't see his face, he knew the man had a scar that cut a pink river through his beard, from eye to jawbone. This was the man who had killed Juana.

"Send him out, Sheriff!" the man called, his horse bucking and moving in fevered circles, as if it wanted to get rid of its rider and make a break for Mexico. "Save your town a whole lotta grief."

"Not gonna happen," Watson called back.

Three more shots followed, two of which came through the window on Tezcat's side of the room, and he hit the floor just as shards of glass rained over him. The third bullet pierced the door and skittered across the floor into the empty jail cell.

"That was your one warning, Sheriff," the rider called out. "You made my day. Me and the boys are gonna love tearin' you and your friends apart. We'll be watching outside town. You try to move him, we'll know. You try to run, we'll know."

"I'm pissing," Watson yelled back, but Tezcat saw the fear in his eyes.

"It's the full moon tonight, Sheriff," the rider shouted. "I can feel it already. You're gonna die, Sheriff. Slow. Slower than those two Mexican bitches we took the other day. You'll see, Sheriff."

Tezcat stood and moved toward the window in a red haze of fury. He drew his gun and fired at the man on the horse. The gun howled, and a funnel of flame blazed from the barrel, but the man had already spurred his mount and was gunning it for the west end of town. A moment passed; Tezcat's blood cooled, and he was filled back up with the sense of emptiness he had lived under since the day he lost his family. He slid to his knees and fell against the wall, his heart pounding. He looked out the way the rider had gone, and he could see stone-colored clouds moving toward town, and in the distance, rough winds had swept up a fog of sand that obscured the horizon. And kneeling there staring out at that dark, whirling wall closing in, he thought he might be ready to kill a man after all. At least these few.

He got to his feet, turned to face the room, and saw that Watson, Andréa, and the Englishman were staring at him, eyes wide. After a moment of confused silence, he realized what they were looking at: the chambers of his pistol were emitting that purple glow again, but this time the light was so full and bright, the shape of the gun was almost completely obscured; it appeared as though he was holding a ball of purple fire. The barrel was glowing orange-hot, as if he'd stuck it into a blacksmith's forge.